JOHNNYKIN AND THE GOBLINS.

Johnnykin and THE GOBLINS

BY CHARLES G. LELAND

ILLUSTRATED BY THE AUTHOR

LONDON

MACMILLAN & CO.

1877

Facsmile edition published by Arabi Manor, a
Rebel Satori imprint
www.arabimanor.com

Originally published 1876

CONTENTS.

CHAPTER I.

PAGE

HOW JOHNNYKIN TALKED WITH THE STONE IMAGE—OF THE
DONKEY THAT WAS TURNED INTO A BOY, AND THE CHERUB
THAT FLEW OUT OF THE TOMBSTONE 9

CHAPTER II.

HOW JOHNNYKIN SANG WITH AN OWL—THE GOBLIN SPELLING-
BEE AND THE QUEEN OF THE DOLLS 26

CHAPTER III.

MARJOLAINE AND CHESMÉ THE CAT-GIRL—FAIRY RIDDLES—THE
DARK TOWER—CHILDE ROLAND AND FRIAR BACON—JOHNNY-
KIN GETS HIS OWN LIFE AND ADVENTURES 58

CHAPTER IV.

GOBLIN LAND AND THE FINGER-MEN—THE SLATE-PENCIL PEOPLE
AND THE DYING BRIGAND—PETER PUMPKIN-EATER, ESQ.—
THE RUSH FAIRIES—CHESMÉ ON A BROOM—HOW JOHNNYKIN
FOUGHT THE KNIGHTS AND SLEW THE PIG—MARJOLAINE
COMES AGAIN 90

PAGE

CHAPTER V.

THE GOBLIN MEETING—THE CHURCH MOUSE—LITTLE BOY BLUE
AND CHARLEY CAKE-AND-ALE WITH HIS TRICKS AND JOKES—
FAIRY FORTUNE-TELLING—WILLIE WINKIE—THE ABSURD
AND THEIR SONGS—HOW OLD BOGEY WENT BACK TO THE
COAL-CELLAR 127

CHAPTER VI.

THE DREADFUL STUPIDS—THE GOBLIN REPORTS ON MISCHIEF—
THE COMMITTEES ON ORANGE-PEEL AND TIP-CATS—THE
FLYING OYSTERS AND TALKING PICTURES—MR. MANNERS. . 162

CHAPTER VII.

FRIAR BACON AND THE CUP OF KING DJEM-SCHID—THE FAIRY
HARP OF HOP-O'-MY-THUMB—THE HORN OF BALDER—THE
TWO GIRLS BECOME REAL PEOPLE WITH THE GOBLIN AND
OWL 191

CHAPTER VIII.

JOHNNYKIN AWAKES IN THE CHURCH-YARD—HIS UNCLE AND
THE DONKEY-BOY—JOHNNYKIN FINDS HIS FRIENDS AGAIN . 202

ᑕHᗩᑭTEᖇ I.

HOW JOHNNYKIN TALKED WITH THE STONE IMAGE—

OF THE

DONKEY THAT WAS TURNED INTO A BOY,

AND THE

CHERUB THAT FLEW OUT OF THE TOMBSTONE.

IT WAS

A Warm Summer Afternoon,

and Johnnykin sat on a grey tomb by a great

gnarled yew-tree, which looked as if it had been
alive and trying for a thousand years to twist
and wrinkle itself into every queer shape it could
think of. Johnnykin was taking the portrait of
a very odd little stone goblin, which was perched
above a pillar of the old church; and while
he drew away very peacefully, listening to the
bees as they buzzed over the grass, a troop of
wild children, bent on mischief, and headed by
Bill Bowser, the very worst boy in the whole
school, burst into the churchyard.

"Hullo!" roared Bill, "here's old Johnnykin
a-drawin' a pictur'. Let's give him a rollin'!"

"Let's smash his figure for him," cried Sam
Slapps. Saying this he cruelly threw a stone at
the goblin, which, if it had hit, would have
put an end to the image and to this story also.

"Oh fy!" said Johnnykin. "This is very
unkind and cruel. Remember what Milton says:—

> "*He that would knock a statue's nose off,*
> *Ought to be whipped with all his clothes off.*"

"Milton ain't the Stilton," replied the vulgar Sam. "Hurrah boys! let's pelt the graven immidge! That'll break Miss Johnnykin's heart!"

Saying this they all began to pick up stones. But Johnnykin cried out in great alarm,—

"Oh please cease! Think of the changes in history which that little figure has seen. Do you think you ought to be bad because he is not good-looking? Remember what the poet says:—

"*Though yon form appear a Goblin,*
Should you for that be a Snoblin,
Spare, oh spare the crumbling Gob,
Do not pelt him like a snob."

"Let him alone, please do, and I will give you six apples which I have here in a scrip. They have got round rosy cheeks like angels," added Johnnykin, as he took them out.

"All right old fellow," replied the bad boy. "Give us the apples and we won't pelt him till

the next time we want to.   Just a napple apiece.
Sorry we haven't got one for you, Johnnykin!"

Saying this they ran off whooping and looking
like goblins themselves; and then, as they went

farther away, they seemed to Johnnykin like
little black imps, then like impkins, and then
midges sporting and vanishing in the golden sun-
set. And Johnnykin thought Bill looked something

" Like a brown butterfly
Which you see flutter by,
Or a tipsy gipsy with wings on the breeze;
With red leaves of Autumn
When storms have caught 'em
And run them away from their homes in the trees."

Then he began again to copy the face of the
old goblin. But as he drew, Johnnykin became
bewildered, for do what he could the likeness
got worse and worse.

"Well, now," he said, sadly vexed. "I've
rubbed it out and drawn it over six times, and
it's not a bit like him. Why I declare!—the face
is changing!"

And sure enough a new colour came over the
stone image as if the last sun-light had just passed
into it and made it alive. And its shape, too,
became different. Its nose was as unlike the one
Johnnykin had drawn as could be, and the whole
figure was thinner.

"I really think," said Johnnykin at last to

the Goblin, just as if it had been alive, "that your face is the same no longer."

"Certainly not," replied the Goblin, in the most natural manner. "It is much shorter."

"Your cheeks were more dilated, I think, Sir," said the boy.

"Yes. Now they're diluted. Thinner, you know," replied the Goblin, with a grin. "Can you tell why I'm so reduced?" he added.

"No, Sir," answered Johnnykin.

"It's because I'm coming down in the world," said the Goblin with a wink. "Down to you. Don't you see? Whenever I get out of my regular respectable place up here, as I intend doing now, and come down to your level, of course I'm no longer a Swell."

Johnnykin could not understand whether the Goblin was trying to be funny or whether he was rude, for all this was spoken in such quiet tones, and with such a droll expression of the eyes, that if he had judged by looks alone he would have thought the image polite enough. So he merely looked at it gravely, and said,

" There once was a Man in a Wall
Came very near getting a fall,
For some very bad boys
Who were making a noise,
Tried to crush that poor Man in the Wall.

But a boy with a bag full of fruit
Persuaded the rest not to do 't :
' Such conduct,' thought he,
' It is easy to see,
Is quite unbecoming a brute.'

And all of his fruit he resigned, to
Just rescue the Man he was kind to,
So that Man can now go
As high or as low
As ever the Man has a mind to."

As Johnnykin repeated this, the Goblin's eyes opened wider, looking as green and bright as emeralds, the corners of his mouth drew down, and he stared at the boy for a long time. It was all one to Johnnykin, who kept his great blue eyes fixed on the Goblin's green ones as if he too were a statue.

"I say!" cried the Goblin suddenly. "Who's going to speak first."

"You spoke first," replied Johnnykin. "If this is a game, Sir, you've lost."

"I believe I did, Johnnykin," said the Goblin, very slowly,—"and I certainly owe you for the apples. You acted very well in that affair by saving my head and giving all you had for my ransom. As the proverb says, 'Handsome is as ransom does.'"

"Yes," cried Johnnykin, very much pleased at this praise, "as one may say,

> *"Though apples were the cause of death,*
> *Yet they have given life to thee,*
> *Since what takes life has spared thy breath,*
> *Thou'rt cured by Homœopathy."*

"Johnnykin," said the Goblin, "it can't be denied—you're a character, and you're fond of poetry."

"I'm afraid I am, and I'm very sorry for it—and so is my Uncle," answered Johnnykin. "He says he will turn me out of the house if I repeat any more verses—and I can't help it, Sir, indeed I can't. And he wants me to be like Bill and the other boys; and indeed, Sir, I'm very unhappy," said poor Johnnykin, looking at the Goblin with tears; for as he had saved the old figure from being broken, and as the Goblin seemed good-natured, it just came into his head that he might get some good advice, and perhaps some help out of his troubles.

"So you would like to have a different sort of life, Johnnykin," said the Goblin. "Well, why shouldn't you? I don't think you're of much use to anybody in that home of yours,— and, what's of far more consequence, there is nobody in it of the slightest use to you. I dare

B

say they'd like to be rid of you altogether, and
I shouldn't wonder if they thought you were
out of your mind—*non compos mentis*, you
know."

"Yes, Sir," said Johnnykin. "Those are
the very words; just what my Uncle said this
morning. And he told me he wished I never
would darken his doors again, because I make
rhymes, just as my father used to, and draw
as my dear mother did—and have so little
sense." And here Johnnykin not knowing that
he was rhyming, began to say with tears in his
eyes—

> "Where have thy wits gone wandering,
>   Sweet heart, this summer day?
>   Have they like geese been squandering
>   Their time among the hay,
>   Where blossoms blow,
>   And grasses grow
>   So merrily all away?
>
> "Oh, if I knew where my wits had gone,
>   I'd surely let thee know,

'Tis better they should go astray
Than have no wits to go.
So there, Sweet heart,
Thou'st got thy part,
And plenty too I trow,"

"I hope, Sir," he continued, "that you won't consider me a stupid boy."

"No, Johnnykin, I don't. Some day you may live among people who will be astonished to know that you were once supposed to be troubled with such a disorder. But come now—listen. To-night we have the Annual Meeting of the Grand Order of Goblins in this church. Would you like to see it?"

"Oh! I should indeed," cried Johnnykin. "I know I should improve my mind. But Uncle has told me I must never stay out later than nine o'clock. As the poet says,

"'*To stay too late with him's a crime,*
We may not heed the hours,
But shall, when we find out in time,
A switch behind the flowers.

B 2

Thus naughty boys who truant play,
Should think before they go—
The brightest blossoms of their day
Upon a birch may grow.'"

"Not quite right, Johnnykin, my boy," said the Goblin, "but well enough for poetry. Now, to business. Your Uncle and friends all think you are a young donkey, while the truth is, if you only were one, they would be quite fond of you. That is all the trouble, and the only trouble. Now I think we can make matters right all round. Look over there—beyond the bushes—what do you see?"

Johnnykin looked, and through the dusk saw a young donkey gazing at him from between two spectral tombstones.

"This young gentleman," said the Goblin, "must help us, Johnnykin. He must go home in your place."

With this he slid down from *his* place, and, coming towards Johnnykin, took his lead-pencil,

which he pointed and waved at the animal. The
effect was very strange, for sparkles of green and
red light rayed forth over the donkey. And as

they rayed, the donkey brayed; but while he was
doing so his form changed, and he stood there the
very image of Johnnykin himself.

"Well, young gentleman," exclaimed the Goblin to the transformed donkey, "do you know what you're wanted for?"

"Yes," replied the donkey-Johnnykin, "I do. I was a-listening all the time. I'm going to be a Boy. Capital idea—'specially for me."

"Perhaps you think," said the Goblin, "that all this is got up merely for your benefit. Well—think so. That's the sort of youth we want you to be. Now—*go!*"

"Any partin' advice, Old Gentleman?" asked the Donkey coolly, as he cocked his hat to suit his new state of mind, and put his hands into his side-pockets.

"Yes—be what you were always, and you'll be happy."

And off went the Donkey. He had said very little, but his every motion and word showed that he was very unlike poor Johnnykin, and that he was very much like Bill and a great many other boys. He was not nice at all, and there was No Nonsense about him.

"It would be lucky, Johnnykin," said the Goblin, as the Donkey vanished in the darkness, "if a great many people were even as well represented as you are. Donkeys are nice enough in their places on the Commons—and sometimes *in* the Commons—under a good Whip. Excuse me for a moment," he added, "while I write a message."

Saying this, he picked up a dead leaf and gave it a slide between his hands, when it came out a post-card. Hastily writing a line, he looked about him for an instant, until his eye lit on a tomb, on which was carved a very queer and ugly Cherub.

"I say—come out of that!" he cried to the carving.

Out came the Cherub, fluttering about in zigzags, like a great moth in the fast-growing darkness.

"Stop that!" said the Goblin. "Keep quiet, can't you?"

The Cherub paused, giving little starts now and then.

"'Take this card, and be off with you!" said the Goblin; "and if you loiter by the way I'll report you to the Post-Master."

"I won't so much as get on my feet, or sit down an instant to rest before I return," said the Cherub, smiling.

"I wonder how he could do it, even if he wanted to!" said Johnnykin, as the messenger went flying over the highest trees.

" That was thought of by a wise man long ago," said the Goblin. " But you don't understand the Cherub, because there's a great difference between you. You're a poet, he isn't. His Sit is on the Wing—your Wit is in the Sing. That's it. Whenever you want to know anything, my dear boy, always come to me."

CHAPTER II.

HOW JOHNNYKIN SANG WITH AN OWL. — THE GOBLIN SPELLING-BEE AND THE QUEEN OF THE DOLLS.

OHNNYKIN and the Goblin sat down on an old tomb The Goblin gave a long soft whistle, when there was all at once a flash of broad wings, and a great owl came sailing round and round them, looking shyly at Johnnykin. At last it sat down close by him in a very friendly way.

"Sporting?" inquired the Goblin.

"Well—yes—a little," replied the Owl.
"I have often read about Owls, Sir," said

Johnnykin, very politely to the visitor, "but I
never made the acquaintance of one before."

"Well—how do you like it, as far as you've got?" asked the Owl.

"Very much, Sir. I have read in one of my school-books that you are always called the Bird of Wisdom."

The Owl cocked his head and winked his eye at the Goblin and said:

"You hear *that*, do you? This young gentleman, who has been carefully educated with the most expensive books, says that everybody calls me the Bird of Wisdom. Well—I *am* up to a thing or two," he said, after a pause.

"And I have heard," said Johnnykin, "that in the old times they put images of Owls into libraries. And Owls are the enemies of mice, because mice injure and destroy books by nibbling them. Mice are the foes of learning."

"How interestin'," said the Owl, "and how improvin' it is to enjoy the conversation of a Scholar. That's what this young gentleman is," he added. "And it's all true what you say, Sir, about mice. Miserable, ignorant little brutes they are. It's awful to think of the books they ruin."

"I know a song, Sir, about an Owl," said Johnnykin.

"Let's hear you sing it," replied the Owl.

"I think I can give the words," said Johnnykin. "But the chorus goes, *Too-whit—too-whoo*—as you sing, Sir——and I couldn't do *that*—very well."

"Well, I can," cried the Owl, "as it's my own natural language; so just you find the body of the song and I'll do the featherin'. I say there," he cried, looking up to the Church. "Come down here, you musicians!"

Johnnykin had often noticed among the carvings on the Church three figures, one holding a harp, the other a lute, and the third a pan-pipe. Down they came at the call, and began to play very sweetly as Johnnykin sang:

THE SONG OF A GERMAN OWL.

" I left my nest in the ivy vine,
The moon was up and the stars did shine,
As I flew away across the Rhine,
And sat on the Tower of Falkenstein.

CHORUS.

" Too-whit—too-whoo !
Oo—hoo—woo-hoo !
Rumty doodely dooden doo."

(Here the Owl, the Goblin, the Musicians, and all the images on the Church, joined in the chorus; and far in the distance, in woods and fields, one owl after another took it up, so that

there was a whoo-hooing as far as the ear
could hear.).

> " *Oh! don't you know the Falkenstein?*
> *The jolly old Owl of Falkenstein;*
> *He has daughters three, divine,*
> *Daughters fair and fat and fine.*

CHORUS.

> " *Too-whit—too-whoo!*
> *Oo—hoo—whoo-hoo!*
> *Rumty doodely dooden doo.*

> " *The eldest girl is Adelaide,*
> *Gertrude is the second maid,*
> *The third one's name you'll have to guess:*
> *There's much we feel we don't express.*

CHORUS.

> " *Too-whit—too-whoo!*
> *Oo-whoo—whoo-hoo!*
> *Rumty doodely dooden doo.*

" *The Owl stood on a mossy wall,*
And there began to hoot and 'call.
The Moon arose, he flapped his wing,
Said he, ' She comes to hear me sing !'

CHORUS.

" *Too-whit—too-whoo !*
Oo-whoo—whoo-hoo !
Rumty doodely dooden doo.

" *The owl upon the bushes sat,*
And when it rained it spoiled his hat,
The sun came out; said he, ' Oh bosh !
It's all the better for a wash !'

CHORUS.

" *Too-whit—too-whoo !*
Oo-whoo—whoo-hoo !
Rumty doodely dooden doo."

"I will keep it up with an old English song : "
said the Owl—

" *Of all the birds that ever I see,*
 The Owl is the fairest in her degree:
 For all the day long she sits in a tree,
 And when the night comes away flies she.
        Too-whit—too-whoo
        Sir Knave—and thou!
 This song is well sung I make you avow;
 And its bill—bill—terrible bill,
 Oh! what do you do with that terrible bill?
 Rats, and rabbits, and mice I kill,
 And that's what I do with this terrible bill."

The eyes of the Owl grew larger and rounder
with delight as he sang. Then the Goblin whistled
again, when Johnnykin hearing a rustling and
clattering, saw by the moonlight that the great
gurgoyles or stone spouts through which rain
pours from the church roof, and which were odd
monsters in form, having become animated, were
climbing down the lead pipes, while the mascarons,
whose heads were the only parts of them visible,
were drawing themselves out of the walls in which
they had been buried up to their necks—leaving

holes behind them to mark their spots. These all knew Johnnykin, for he had often taken their portraits, and as none of them had ever paid him for doing so, they treated him in the most amiable manner.

"This gentleman," said the Goblin, turning towards a Gurgoyle, who had just joined their party, and whom Johnnykin remembered as having been perched on the very top of the tower, "is the only one who occupies a very high position among us. He is a High Churchman—and very eloquent. You ought to hear him pour forth. In fact," he added, gravely, "he has been spouting on the Church side, ever since the days of King Stephen—yes, and during every reign at that."

I don't know what the Gurgoyle would have replied to this beautiful compliment, had not the Goblin suddenly proposed a Spelling Bee, to pass the time until the great meeting should begin. So they all four sat down around the old tomb.

"Can you spell well, my dear?" asked the Goblin of Johnnykin.

"*W—e—l—l*," he answered.

"Very good. That is a double answer, so I shall give you some double spelling. How do you spell *charitable?*" he continued.

"C—h—a—r—i—t——

"Dear! dear! no. That will never do."

"How do *you* spell it, Sir?" asked Johnnykin.

"Why, with three letters—the same that are used in *hat*," was the reply.

"I really don't understand you," said Johnny-kin, staring.

"Look here!" said the Goblin. The four —that is the Owl, the Goblin, the Gurgoyle, and Johnnykin—were seated each with one side of the old grey tomb before him, as if at whist. The Goblin took out a piece of chalk, and drew on the slab the following:

h

"There," he exclaimed, "that's a chair—isn't it?"

"Yes, Sir," replied Johnnykin.

"And this is the letter *a?*" he added drawing again.

a

"Of course."

"And this is a table?"

T

"Yes."

"Well then, my dear, look at this—

h a T

and tell me if it doesn't spell chair-a-table? That's the way we Goblins always spell it."

"It's very ingenious," replied Johnnykin, "but can you prove it's quite the right way?"

"Of course it's right," said the Owl. "Don't they al'ays pass round a hat for charity, supposin' there's no plate?"

Johnnykin was quite bewildered at this, and the Goblin went on.

"Talking of chairs and tables, can you spell bedstead?"

Johnnykin began with "*B—e—d——*" but was interrupted.

"Too much, too much! This is our way, of spelling it Johnnykin, my dear." Saying this the Goblin drew this very long H—

⊢⊣

"But," said Johnnykin, "I object to such a method, because——"

"Of course you do," said the Gurgoyle, "and so you ought. Don't you see that this is what

is called Object teaching by which Objects are
substituted for letters. The teacher objects, and
of course the scholars ought to."

Johnnykin looked steadily at him, but said
nothing.

"The trouble in your case, Johnnykin," said
the Goblin, "is that you did not begin rightly
from the beginning. I don't suppose you even
know your Alphabet as you should. You use
too many letters. Now how many are there?"

"Twenty-six, Sir."

The Goblin shook his head very sadly, and
there was a murmur of grief from all present.

"Too many, *too* many;" he sighed. "No,
Johnnykin—there are only twelve. For instance,"
he said, taking his chalk and drawing a letter
on the tomb, and in the centre, "what's this?"

ɯ

"I should call it an old M," said Johnnykin.

"Now to me it looks like an old W," said the
Owl, who sat opposite.

ɯ

"I call it a B," cried the Gurgoyle.

ℬ

"And I an E," added the Goblin.

ℰ

"But we are all quite right," he added—"all *quite* right. So you will observe if you please that

p q d b

are all the same letter."

"That is making four out of one," said Johnnykin, who was much interested in this new method.

"Exactly. Quartering it as one may say. But the letter which you quarter is the double W, with which you began."

❀

"So you see that the seven letters are all really one, for there are p b d and q again, only a little

changed by time. Then you can make five out
of one letter if you're not too particular as to
shape—and none of these gentlemen are, I
believe—"

The Owl and the Gurgoyle bowed very low,
to show that they quite agreed with him.

"Well—take N. What does that make?"

$$ N \quad Z \quad S \quad N $$

"Why N, Z, and S, of course. The last letter
is the combination of V and A. You may
remember it by Victoria and Albert."

"But the A isn't crossed," said Johnnykin.

"No more it ought to be," said the Owl.
"Albert never was crossed in anything that ever
I heard of. And that none of 'em ever may be
is my lovin' prayer," he loyally added.

"Well," said the Goblin, "if you please to
look at a and ɒ or c and d as one letter,
you will find yourself much better off than
before."

"Ever so much better," said the Owl. "Quite convalescent as the doctors say. In fact after all that I feel wonderfully like sittin' up and takin' a little nourishment," he added, looking at the Goblin with a grin.

The latter replied by taking the chalk and drawing the letter Y four times on the tomb, for four wine glasses.

Y Y Y Y

He then made a mark in each to show that they contained liquid,

Y Y Y Y

and then *picked up* each with his fingers and presented it as a real glass full of wine to the company.

The Owl smacked his bill as he drank. Johnnykin thought he had never tasted anything so nice.

"Good wine, Johnnykin my boy?" asked the Goblin. "It's worth while being a man of letters, isn't it, when you can turn your letters to such account?"

"What do you call the wine?" asked Johnnykin.

"Vin de Grave—of course," replied the Goblin. "Didn't you see I got it out of the tomb?"

"I think, Sir," said Johnnykin, "I understand how you got the glasses." He hadn't the remotest idea in reality, you know, but his droll little mind was always fancying something. "But I can't understand how you got the wine into them."

"Dear me!" said the Gurgoyle, "that's very simple. Didn't you see that he *drew* it? Did you never hear of drawing wine before? There are a great many people who draw all their wine and beer too from the tavern by means of chalk-marks. I knew a man once," he added very slowly, as if thinking over old times, "named Rip Van Winkle, who drew thousands of pounds' worth of liquor in that way."

"If he drank so much he must have been very sleepy after it," said Johnnykin.

"So he was. He slept twenty-five years. I saw him asleep myself."

"And I shall be sleepy myself," said the Owl, "unless I have a pipe. I say," he added, turning to the Goblin, "couldn't you find some tobacco?"

The Goblin replied by taking his chalk and drawing a letter

P

Taking this up, he rolled out the stem on the stone and bent it a little after drawing it out into this shape:

This made a very good pipe. He then drew a bird with a very large eye. "This," he said, "is what is called a Bristol bird."

Taking the bird up, the Owl filled his pipe from it.

"How is it that you find tobacco there, Sir?" asked Johnnykin.

"Don't you see it is Bird's Eye?" replied the Owl.

Johnnykin said nothing, but he could not help thinking that his Uncle would have liked to know such a cheap and easy way of obtaining his tobacco. He then took another sip of the wine, finding it nicer than before, and held it up as he had seen grown-up gentlemen do, and thought it looked very pretty in the moonlight, and then saw a star shine through it which made a very pretty fairy bee's-wing; when all at once he observed something very curious, which was that the glass was as full as ever. He at once inquired the reason of this.

"Ah, Johnnykin, my boy," replied the Goblin, "I'm afraid you are very ignorant. Don't you know that every liquid always keeps its proper level, owing to the pressure of the atmosphere?"

"I have heard so," answered Johnnykin, after thinking a little.

"Well—and isn't the proper level of a glass-ful of wine, the brim?"

"*I* should say so," remarked the Owl. "No short measure for *me*."

"Very good. Therefore the wine in every honest glass never gets below the brim. Honest glasses are full-sized ones. This Johnnykin, is what is called a Law of Hydrostatics, and as a good citizen I consider it my duty to see that the law is never broken."

"Until the glasses is," remarked the Owl, very solemnly. Johnnykin observed that the Owl had been testing the law very thoroughly ever since he had received the glass.

"I am sure," said Johnnykin, "that I am very grateful to you for telling me all this. But I should like to know how it is that I am able to see all these wonders, when other people cannot?"

"The reason is," replied the Goblin, "that you are spiritual-eyesed. You don't know much about spelling," he added gloomily. "How are you at arithmetic?"

"If it's to be Goblin arithmetic?" exclaimed Johnnykin.

"Of course it is. There's no fun in common arithmetic. Now answer. How many do you and I make?"

"Two," answered Johnnykin.

"No. We make one hundred and one trillions, one hundred and eleven billions, two hundred and one millions, eight hundred and fourteen thousand, two hundred and twenty two. See here!"

And with his chalk the Goblin wrote it out thus :—

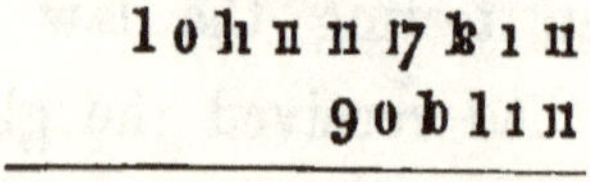

1 o h n n ꞁ7 ƀ ı ıı

9 o b l ı ıı

—————————————

101,111,201,814,222

"Those are our names, and as they are made of figures, of course they are correct, and add up."

"Then you must have a whole alphabet of figures," said Johnnykin.

"Of course; and here it is," answered the Goblin :—

α b ꞓ d e ᒋ 9 h ı Ƅ l ɯ ıı o p q ı s � ıı

ɯ ⅄ 7 3

"Now, our old people say that if you write your name out according to this figure alphabet it will show how many farthings you will spend, if you have the luck to get them. But, according to others, it gives the number of seconds you'd like to live. And some say it sets forth the number of foolish wishes you'll make, and

when you've made the last one you'll be happy.
You see by this, however," he added, "that
spelling and arithmetic are all the same thing.
It saves ever so much time to learn them both
together. That's the reason our children have
so many holidays; they learn everything at once
and altogether in one lesson. But look out !" he
cried, hastily, "here's the company coming!"

As he said this, there was a distant rushing as
of many wings, and the sound of light voices far
away, and then a fairy chorus as delicate as if the
night-flowers were singing, while with it rang
soft bell-tones like church chimes and lute and
flute music, all as merry and mad as could be.
And then came a sudden shout and a fluttering and
whirring high in the air overhead, and then silence,
broken by one loud peal of solitary laughter.
And then Johnnykin saw many strange shadowy
forms, lighting and leaping on the top of the old
Church Tower. In an instant hundreds came
rustling through the ivy, head over heels,
rollicking and frolicking like wild school-children,

while others floated downwards soft as snow-
flakes, or wavering up and away, or far about
in fancy flights like fragments of paper or gold
leaf when you let them fall from a high
window.

The funniest little figures, which looked
like mannikins or babies among the rest, were
also the jolliest, and Johnnykin noticed that all
the Cupids in the country, from churches or houses,
old or new, all the odd little creatures from choir-
seats, and all the droll mannikins in every kind
of carving had come to life, and were swarming
in by thousands. This army of weenie youngsters
was under the command of a beautiful lady with
very long flowing curling hair, which in the
strange light kept changing colour from silver
flaxen to gold, auburn, gold-brown, dark brown,
and black. Her face was as lovely and kind
as could be. With her bare arms and beautiful
hands she directed and swept all her wild little
flock wherever she willed, without speaking a
word to them or touching them.

D 2

As she came near Johnnykin, he bowed politely to her, and she smiled and said:

"So we have a real boy here to night. I am the Queen of the Mannikins. I rule all the toys and little images that men make."

"If you please, Your Majesty," said Johnnykin, "how is it that they come to life?"

"All images, and many other things that men make or handle or live with, get a kind of life from man. Sometimes this life awakes, and then they frolic about in secret, and imitate their masters and mistresses. When a nice little doll has been nursed a great deal by a bright little girl, and talked to and instructed, do you suppose it is all lost and wasted? No indeed. Dolly remembers it all, and some night it is all shown."

"Is there any way to make images or dolls alive?"

"Certainly. Whenever a girl or boy— particularly a boy—has been *perfectly good* all day long, and learned every lesson and teased

nobody, and been very polite and used only
the best language, and not listened to other
people's conversation, it may be done; for such
magic deeds can only be worked by very pure
people. Then the girl or boy, before going to
bed, must put one finger on the figure or doll,
and say this :—

> "' *Moon—shine on me!*
> *Life come into thee!*
> *As much as I was good to-day,*
> *So much may you arise and play.*
> *By the bee in the bell,*
> *And the sun on the stream,*
> *You may wake, and may walk, and may talk while*
> *I dream.'*

"And then the doll will get up and walk in
the night. But as for seeing what they do, that
can only be done in dreams, and even for that
the children must have been *very* good indeed.
Good-bye—we must now attend to the opening
song."

There was a sudden silence, almost as she spoke and then all those present sang this,—

" The Rose leaned over the garden wall,
The Pebble sat by the water-fall ;
' Come out of your stone !
It is time to be gone,

While the Poppy is red and the Corn is green,
And the Blue Fly sings to the Celandine;
    And while I blow,
    And waters flow,—
Up flies the Fairy, and off they go!

" The Night Hawk sat on the forest stone,
And called to the Elf, who lived alone;
' Come out of your cave, and let us begone!'
' Oh no—for here is a hatchet of stone,
A knife of bronze, and a needle of bone,
' Which I must watch.'—' Never mind—come on!
For I asked for leave—and He said you may!'
Out jumped the Elf, and they hurried away.

" And the Pitcher called to the Yellow Frog,
' Come to the garden and leave the bog!
By the Blackberry-wire and Dead-wood fire,
For the Lily may rest when the Bramble must tire!
And the Silver Mouse is waiting for you!'
Flop came the Frog, and away they flew.

" And the Dolls which the children left asleep,
Wake up and away to the window creep;

For every one has a fairy beau,
Or a fairy sweetheart, as you know,
And away the dolls and the fairies go!
Off in the night,
By the light of the star,
Over the chimney-pots—ever so far!

" Rose, and Fairy, and Frog, and Doll,
Elves, and Pitchers, and Birds and all,
Goblins, Squirrels, and Pinks, and Rats,
Spoons, and Lilies, and Bees, and Cats,

Tongs, and Dormice, and Toys, and Bats,
Everything that can fly or walk,
Everything that can dance or talk,
You and I and all are free
    To come to the Goblins' Jubilee."

CHAPTER III.

MARJOLAINE AND CHESMÉ THE CAT-GIRL—FAIRY
RIDDLES—THE DARK TOWER—CHILDE ROLAND
AND FRIAR BACON—JOHNNYKIN GETS HIS OWN
LIFE AND ADVENTURES.

T seemed very strange to Johnnykin
that wherever he walked the great
crowd of Shining Ones was always
circling round and round him:
so that he could not help
remembering how he had been
shown that a light cast on a
looking-glass or a pane which has received
millions of little invisible scratches by being

often rubbed, always seems to be in the centre of a circle of little gleams. He was separated from his friends, and was just beginning to wonder what to do, when all at once there stepped from the procession which swept so grandly about him, a young girl, who looked at him for a moment, and then said:

"Don't you know me? I am Marjolaine de Montfort."

Johnnykin remembered her at once as the beautiful little lady in white marble on the old tomb in the church, where she knelt on a broad tablet. But there she was only marble, with a few remains of gilding in the embroidery of her dress, while now she glowed and blushed as if a kind of very delicate Northern light were waving and flitting through her features.

"You know," said Marjolaine, "that you are the only real boy who is here. I used to be a real girl myself once—but that was—oh! ever so long ago. If you would like to go outside," she added timidly, "you might have better fun than you find in all this horrid noise."

"Thank you," said Johnnykin. "I would so much like to walk out with you in the moonlight."

"Ah—you must do something more dashing than that," said Marjolaine smiling. "Would you do something very bold for a lady—for *me*?"

"Indeed I would," said Johnnykin, who had never in his life seen any one half so beautiful as this girl, or with such a sweet manner.

Marjolaine bent her head a little and looking at him with a droll smile in her lovely eyes, said :—

> "*There were Three Brethren out of Spain,*
> *Who came to court Fair Marjolaine.*
> *Fair Marjolaine was far too young,*
> *She had no skill in flattering tongue;*
> *And so to her each Knight did say,*
> '*We will return another day.'*
>
> "*Now Johnnykin shall be my Knight,*
> *And with those Spanish Brethren fight,*
> *And if you fight and conquer too,*
> *I'll come o'er hill and dale to you;*
> *And you will never fight in vain,*
> *If you but think of Marjolaine.*"

"It is all like an old story-book," thought Johnnykin. It did not seem in the least strange to him that he should be told to go after

adventures, and fight for a young lady by way
of amusing himself out of doors for a few minutes.
He only said :

"I will do anything you ask. But will you
be so kind as to tell me where I'm to go?"

"Oh—just follow Chesmé," said Marjolaine.
"Here she is."

As she spoke, there came to them the queerest
creature Johnnykin had ever seen. At first it had

a pretty girl's face on the body of a great cat,
yet while he was looking, the whole changed very
quickly to a girl, and a very wild gipsy girl too.
But in a few seconds she had a cat's face, and
then the body became a cat's; but she was scarcely
all cat before her head and neck became those of
a goose; and so she went on changing to an
entire goose, and then to something else, at times
half one animal, and half another, and then a
whole one.

"What a droll being it is, to be sure," said
Johnnykin.

"Oh—you mean Chesmé," said Marjolaine, as
if Chesmé had been the most ordinary creature
in the world. "Chesmé's a dear, good thing—
she'll do anything, or turn herself into Anything
to oblige me; that is to say, anything you know
except a mouse or a fox, or whatever don't agree
with her. Here, Chesmé!" she said, "show this
young gentleman the way. And," she whispered
to Johnnykin, with a pleasant little smile, "be sure
and know me again when we meet. Dear m'

I had almost forgotten something! We must all be at the Great Meeting when it begins—and that will be in ten minutes. But never mind. Just take this ring. Every time you turn it, it will make a second seem an hour. Don't forget!"

Chesmé as a Goose

Marjolaine was gone as she spoke the last word.

"If you would be so kind as to show me the way," he said to Chesmé, who stood by as a great goose. She began at once to change to a goose-cat, a cat, a cat-rabbit, a rabbit-ferret, and so on, until she was a girl, and a very fine girl too. She made these changes so rapidly, that as fast as she threw aside one form and took another, Johnnykin could still perceive the old ones, at first distinctly, and then vanishing.

"If I don't happen to be a girl when you speak to me," said Chesmé, "you must wait, you know, till I come round to it. Come on!"

"What a beautiful large cat you are," said Johnnykin. "Is that the kind they call Persian?"

"Yes," said Chesmé, very much pleased. "We are the finest cats in the world. I come from Persia. I was born in a fountain, and Chesmé is the Persian word for one. All over that country and Turkey people show you fountains which are inhabited by Chesmé cats, which are only seen by moonlight, and then appear as beautiful girls, who smile all the time, and then vanish quickly into other forms, as you have seen me do.

E

mother's name was Empusa. She was a Greek.
Ah ! you ought to have seen her change !"

Saying this she went on very rapidly, with
Johnnykin at her side, leading him by the

hand through the gloom, until they came out
into full moonlight and to a very broad ditch,
on the other side of which rose a high, thick
hedge.

"Are you good at jumping?" she asked Johnnykin.

"Pretty good."

"Then follow my leader!" cried Chesmé, with a laugh; and, changing to a cat, she made a clear leap over the great ditch, and, hitting the hedge in the centre, seemed to vanish in it.

"Well! what are you waiting for?" Johnnykin heard her cry from the other side. "Why
don't you jump? Hurry along!"

Johnnykin hesitated. Just beside him was
a Mile-Stone. As he looked at it the Mile-Stone
seemed to take the face of an old Labourer.

"It's nothin' if you ain't afraid, Master," said
the Mile-Stone, in an encouraging whisper. "Give
yourself a good fling, now! Only don't go too
high! *That's* a man! Hep! hep! One—two—
three!"

And with *three* Johnnykin sure enough went
flying. "I may as well try," he thought; and

try he did, and that so hard that he went like a sky-rocket clear. over the hedge, high in the air, and came down like the stick on Chesmé, both rolling over and over, she being at the time a Goose. She began at once to go through her changes, and when she was a girl again, said:

"Don't try so hard next time. It's enough if you only *wish* it, you know. You should only try hard when Something's after you, such as a fox, or a dog, or a hunter, or a poacher."

Just then they came to a tree. Chesmé said to it:

"I want to find the Dark Tower."

"All right," replied the Tree. "Right up you come, and then go straight forwards."

Chesmé turned into a cat, and flew up the trunk, and called to Johnnykin to follow. The Tree was a very tall oak, with a straight, smooth trunk.

"Well—what are you waiting for?" said the oak, as if astonished. "Can't you walk on a smooth road?"

"Don't scold him," cried Chesmé, from the tree. "Jump now—quick!"

"I'm sure I don't know how I'm to go up," said Johnnykin. But gentle as he was he had plenty of pluck, and he knew he was expécted to follow Chesmé. So with a bound he flew at the tree, and found himself up in the forks in an instant.

"Now follow me!" said Chesmé.

They were walking along a road in the dark, and she was holding his hand. Little by little there came more moonlight.

· "I wonder where on earth or out of the earth I am now," said Johnnykin. "But it's a riddle, I suppose, without an answer."

"Do you know anything about riddles?" cried Chesmé, very quickly. "Oh! how I wish you did!"

"I can find out the answers to a great many," Johnnykin replied.

"Oh! that's all nonsense," said Chesmé. "Anybody can find out an answer to a riddle. What I want is to find out the riddle to an answer. Don't you know how it is here in Goblin Land? We poor things begin by being stones, and then vegetables, and then fish, and then animals. Then they give us riddles to find the answers, and oh! they're a hundred thousand times harder than any you real boys and girls ever heard of. Well, after we've found them all out, we become what I am now, human part of the time and animal the rest. Then they give us an Answer, and tell us to find out the Riddle to it. Now I have been trying for years to find one out. The answer is the Year — and I've made more than four thousand riddles to it, but none of them will do. Now, if a real person were of his free will to help us it would be allowed, but we goblins mustn't help one another."

"Let me hear one of your riddles," said Johnnykin, who was very much interested.

"Certainly. This is my best one. Our Riddle Master says that it is all right but three words :—

> "*Twelve men very old,*
> *Six hot and six cold,*
> *Some thirty children own,*
> *Others have thirty-one,*
> *To one we twenty-eight assign,*
> *Though sometimes he has twenty-nine.*"

"Oh ! I can see where *that* is wrong," cried Johnnykin ; "at least I think I do."

"What is it?" cried Chesmé, very quickly.

"Why, you begin by saying—

" *Twelve* men *very old*."

"Now, I have often heard it said that the month of March is a woman."

"Can you prove it?" asked Chesmé.

"There's an old fairy tale which says so," replied Johnnykin.

"Then it *must* be true!" cried Chesmé, delighted.

"Yes. Once upon a time there was a traveller, who came in the night to a lonely place among some rocks, where he found eleven men and a woman sitting round a fire. And the woman had a dog, whose head was like a lion's but its body like a lamb."

"I see," said Chesmé. "It came in like a lion, but went out like a lamb, and looked like one of those shaved French Poodles."

"Yes. That's the way it behaved too. And they all began to talk about the weather—it was

in March, you know.   And the traveller said,
'Most people abuse the month of March, but
for my part I like it very much indeed.   All
the year depends on March.'   When the woman
heard that she smiled.   And from that night he

always had good fortune, especially in March.
When he was attacked by robbers, there came
a great storm and rain, which washed his enemies
away; and when he was poor there came a

tremendous wind, which blew down a rock, and he
found a pot of gold; and when he was cold the

sun shone and warmed him. At last one day he
fell into a river and was drowning, but Somebody

threw him her long hair and drew him ashore, and
he saw it was the woman he had met among the
rocks with the eleven men.   And she said, 'Do
you know who I am?   I am the Month of
March, and I have been good to you, because
you spoke well of me.'   Now, if March is
a woman, your riddle ought to begin like
this :

'Eleven men, a woman, old.'"

"Found!   found!" cried Chesmé, clapping
her hands, and leaping with joy.   "Now I shall
be a girl *all* the time.   Good-bye, Pussy Cat!
good-bye, Goose!   And I do thank you *so*
much!—oh! so very much!" she cried, to
Johnnykin.

"I like fairy tales very much," she said, as
she went on, "only they're so improbable, you
know, and I don't like that at all."

"That seems to me to be very odd," replied
Johnnykin.   "Why you're a Fairy Girl yourself."

"Yes—and that's just the reason. You real boys and girls like to hear improbable stories about fairies, but we in Fairyland like to hear probable stories about real children."

This was such a new idea to Johnnykin, that he kept quiet for some time. Then he said, "I should like to hear one of your stories."

"Certainly," replied Chesmé. "This is one. 'Once upon a time there was a real woman, who had an actual son. When he woke up bodily it was a true morning, and he bathed himself with visible soap in perceptible water, and went down and had some trustworthy tea, and some material muffins and positive butter, with a palpable bloater. Then he walked along a rational road to an unimaginative school, where he learned veritable lessons, all in prose. When he was unquestionably bad he got sound, corporeal punishment with an authentic switch or a reliable rod, and cried unfeigned tears. Then he used to say with accuracy, 'Twice

one is two, twice two is four, twice three is six—
twice—— ' "

"Oh come now!" said Johnnykin; "you don't
call that a Story, do you? Why, you're saying
the Multiplication Table."

"It's such a story as we like to hear," replied
Chesmé, with a sigh, "because it's all so Real."
Then she was silent, and walked on, till after
a while she said:

"Do you notice that thing which has been
walking on before us for ever so long?"

Johnnykin looked, and saw that a tall, dim
form was going on before them, stopping whenever they stopped.

"It's a Giant," said Johnnykin, "but it looks
like a Tower."

"It's the Dark Tower," said Chesmé. "Do
you know why I bring you to it? Here, in
Fairyland, whenever we begin to be dull, and
want to enjoy something which seems quite real,
we have each a book of our own adventures,
and we begin to read in it. And while we

read, the things we are reading about keep
really happening, and we are really living in
them."

"That's very hard to understand," said
Johnnykin.

"Why it seems very simple to me. Don't
you have pictures in your books—you real boys
and girls?"

"Certainly," replied Johnnykin.

"Well — can't you imagine looking at real
things instead of pictures, hearing sounds, and
smelling the flowers in pictures? Now our books
are so well written that when you are reading them you really think you are doing all
this."

"Then I suppose," said Johnnykin, "with
such a book one can have adventures whenever
one pleases. Ah! I should like to have such
a book as that!"

"I knew you would," cried Chesmé, delight-
edly, "and for that reason I'll get you one. I'd
do anything for you. When you go into the

Dark Tower, you'll see Childe Roland, and just ask him if he has got among his books one about yourself. He'll give it to you. It was so nice in you to help me with that riddle," she added.

By this time it had grown lighter, and the Dark Tower was seen very plainly moving on before them.

" Stop ! " cried Chesmé.

" I am only waiting for your commands," said the Tower, respectfully. As he spoke he yawned frightfully, and in so doing opened his door, showing a horrible row of teeth.

" This gentleman must see Childe Roland," said Chesmé. " Tell him to give him what he wants, and charge it to me. Now, good-bye," she said to Johnnykin. " You'll see me again soon. Turn your ring ! "

As she spoke she jumped into a great stone, and vanished. The Dark Tower yawned again. Johnnykin did not like the looks of his mouth at all.

" It's awfully like being eaten alive," he said.

F

"And then the idea of going into a thing like that, which has teeth and talks, you know!"

"I say!" exclaimed the Tower, "you don't

want me to get bronchitis, do you, keeping the wind blowing into my throat, with my mouth open!"

There was no help for it, and Johnnykin ran through the door as fast as he could. It closed with a tremendous snap-bang! He found himself in a beautiful ruined cloister, brightly lit by the moon. All was as silent as it is in Moonland itself, where there are no voices to speak. At the end of the cloister was a tombstone against the wall, and on the upright stone was carved the form of a grim old monk, with a long beard. Johnnykin stopped to look at it.

" Do you want anything?" inquired the Monk.

" 1 want Childe Roland."

" I am he. I was a warrior once. I'm a Monk now," said the old man. And with this he stepped out of his tombstone.

" Does anyone live here with you?" asked Johnnykin.

" Only Friar Bacon—the man who invented gunpowder, you know. Here he is!"

Saying this, another old man entered, and stood by Johnnykin.

"Ah!" he exclaimed, "a Mortal Boy! Mortal Boy—what are the newest inventions on earth? Tell me everything!"

Johnnykin tried to think, and then exclaimed, "Steamboats, locomotive engines, apple-parers, revolvers, paper shirt-collars, Liebig's extract, yeast powder, percussion caps, post-cards, artificial ivory, dynamite, and rinking."

"Ah!" exclaimed the Monk, sadly, "I invented all of those things myself once — yes, Mortal Boy — every one of them, but people didn't want them then. What do you want?" he cried suddenly, as if waking up.

"A book."

"Any book in particular, Mortal Boy?" asked Friar Bacon.

"If you have a copy of *The Adventures of Johnnykin*, I should like to get it."

The Friar went away through a side door, and soon returned with a little parchment-bound book with silver clasps.

"Here—take it!" said the old man, very good-naturedly.

"Stop a minute!" said Childe Roland. "Are you a good mortal boy?" he asked Johnnykin. "Are you honest?"

"I hope so, Sir," replied Johnnykin.

"*Who stole the Donkey?*" inquired the old man, with a piercing look.

"I think, Sir," replied Johnnykin, "that there was no donkey stolen—and secondly, the Goblin did it, and thirdly, that there is no donkey, because he is a boy!"

Johnnykin was almost frightened to find himself talking so boldly, but the old men only smiled.

"It is time for you to go now," said Friar Bacon. "Not through the door, you know, Mortal Boy!" he added; "that only opens to let people in. You must leave by the window!"

Johnnykin looked out of the window. It was very high, and far below it yawned a great ravine, hundreds of feet deep, with steep, rocky sides, here and there covered with old trees, while in the depths he could see a snow-white, foaming torrent, rushing madly along in the clear moonlight, but so very far below that he could hear no sound from it. It was a beautiful prospect, but Johnnykin did not like the prospect of being thrown into it. Meanwhile, the two old Monks had brought a long, narrow plank, which they put half-way out, over the window-sill.

"Now then, Mortal Boy," said Childe Roland, "Good-bye!"

"But," replied Johnnykin, "you don't expect me to walk that plank, and be thrown off?"

"Certainly," said Friar Bacon. "It's a new invention· of mine," he added, proudly, "for seeing visitors out. You walk out to the further end of the plank, and then we two sit down suddenly on *this* end, and then you will be shot —oh! ever so high up!"

"It's quite a Sensation," said Childe Roland.

"Perfectly delightful," added Friar Bacon.

"It cures Neuralgia!" cried Childe Roland.

"We have a great many certificates of its excellency from all the Nobility and Gentry," said Friar Bacon. "Miss Marjolaine de Montfort

is very fond of trying it."

When Johnnykin heard this, he thought he would take the risk. So he hastily ran out to the end of the plank.

"Good-bye, Everything," he said, "if this is to kill me! But I really have got so far now——."

As he said this, the two old men jumped or bumped on the inside end of the plank, and

Johnnykin felt himself shot like a pea from a
blow-pipe high in the air. But, instead of falling violently, he came down like a feather into
the road, and, looking up, saw the Dark Tower
glittering in the moonlight, and the two old
monks waving their hands in friendly farewell
to him from the window.

CHAPTER IV.

GOBLIN LAND AND THE FINGER-MEN—THE SLATE-
PENCIL PEOPLE AND THE DYING BRIGAND—
PETER PUMPKIN-EATER, ESQ.—THE RUSH
FAIRIES—CHESME ON A BROOM—HOW JOHNNY-
KIN FOUGHT THE KNIGHTS AND SLEW THE
PIG—MARJOLAINE COMES AGAIN.

 OHNNYKIN found himself in a very shady
road, but into which the moonlight
often shone through gaps in the trees.
Somehow it seemed as if it must be
always moonlight there. He walked
on, and came to high rocks, and then
to a more open country, but there
seemed to be something strange in
everything. The breeze blowing in

the branches almost played tunes, the leaves as they rustled, giggled and tittered like little girls, and whispered words, and Johnnykin was quite sure he

heard, "That's Johnnykin—he, he, he!" and "Marjolaine," many times. And the rocks looked like things of all kinds—like queer old houses and

towers stuck all over with little towers, like
decanters, and vases, and every kind of enormous
toy and animal he had ever heard of, but all in
weather-worn stone.　At last he passed by a great
pile of books, every one twenty yards long, and
this put him in mind of the one which the monk
had given him.　The moon was so bright that
he could see every letter, so he walked along
reading.　And this was the first sentence of the
first chapter.

"After this Boy, whose name was Jonnikin,
had left the Dark Tower, he came to a right faire
Road, where he began to read in his Book.　And
when he lookt up he saw by the Road-side five
Men who were Brothers, and their Names were,
Corporal Thumbikin, Foreman, Longman, Ringman and Littleman."

Here he stopped reading, and on looking up
really saw five men standing on a rock by the road.
They seemed in the moonlight to be all of one

piece with the rock; they looked, too, as if they were all solid pieces themselves, without arms or legs, and they were staring steadily at him in the moonlight.

"Are you Corporal Thumbikin?" said Johnny-kin to the one who seemed to be their chief.

Thumbikin bowed, but very oddly, for it was backwards, and then he leaned forwards, staring as steadily as before.

"And you are Foreman?" said Johnnykin to the second, "and you Longman, and you two Ringman and Littleman?"

As he spoke they all bowed in the same way, backwards.

"That's an odd way you have of bowing," said Johnnykin.

"Oh, we can do it the other way if you like!" said Foreman. With this the rock and the five men instantly turned around, and as they did so their faces all went to the other side of their heads, and they bowed very low indeed.

"Well!—of *all* the odd things!" said Johnnykin.

"What's odd?" replied Ringman. "Did you never make little faces with pen and ink on your fingers—*in school-time?*" he added in an awful voice, "*when you ought to have been at your lessons?*"

"Yes," answered Johnnykin.

"Sometimes on the nails, and sometimes on t'other side," said Longman, sinking his voice to a fearful whisper.

" Yes."

" And put little paper caps on 'em ? "

" Yes."

" Then you were doing Us," remarked Ringman sternly. " And you didn't think the Hour of Vengeance would approach, and the Wind would blow, and the Feathers would go, and We be on Hand."

" I should think," said Johnnykin, " that you would always be On Hand."

" I say—is that a Joke ? " asked Corporal Thumbikin, in a startled anxious manner, and stooping down towards Johnnykin.

" Yes," replied Johnnykin, very stoutly.

" A *real* joke, such as people laugh at ? Could *we* laugh at it, do you think—ever so much ? "

" Yes—as much as you please."

" He says we may laugh ! " said Thumbikin, with his mouth half open, and both eyes and mouth wearing a wild and startled look. " And as much as we please. I say—*let's* laugh ! But start fair. Now ! One—Two—Three ! "

Saying this the whole five burst into such peals of laughter as Johnnykin had never heard in all his life. They screamed and roared with delight, they all bent themselves double into a clenched fist—they howled and yelled as if in an agony of fun. Then they began again, twisting about and jumping up and down. Johnnykin began to fear they would laugh themselves to death, when he thought of looking into his book. And there he read:

"Now these five men would have laught on for ever, had not Johnnikin said, 'Stopp!'"

"Stop!" he cried.

The five brothers stood up as grave and stupid as ever.

"We never heard a joke before in all our lives," said Thumbikin. "I once heard *part* of a one," he added, "and we always did all our laughing on that. After this we shall always laugh at your joke instead. I say," he added anxiously, "it'll keep—won't it?"

"Yes—as long as you choose to keep it."

"We'll have it on Tuesdays, and Thursdays, and Saturdays, from twelve till ten, and then a little bit of it before going to bed. That won't be too much, will it?"

"Not if you like it," replied Johnnykin. "Good-bye!"

"Good-bye!" they cried, all bowing together, and then stood up with the moonshine full on their flat stupid faces.

As Johnnykin walked on he saw a rock like a very queer house. The roof was like a great copy book in one part and an atlas in another, there was an inkstand for a chimney, out of which smoke kept coming in the shape of a pen, and there were in the garden other inkstands for flower-pots, and in these pen-shaped flowers were growing. There was a tower like a ruler, and a grove of slate-pencils before it. The walls of the house were geographies, and arithmetics, and Latin and French grammars, and the door was an immense slate in a frame.

G

" O dear ! " said Johnnykin, " here's some more school ! "

As he stopped, he saw all kinds of queer

figures hopping out of the slate. They began dancing and frisking about like monkeys before him. They were slaty-grey in colour, and

Johnnykin thought he had seen them all before.
One was a very badly shaped robber or brigand,
holding a sword. He rushed up to Johnnykin
and cried, " *Boo!* "

THE BRIGAND.

" Who are you ? " asked Johnnykin.
" We're the Figures you drew on your slate in
school-time," cried the Robber.

" We're the caricatures you made," screamed another. Johnnykin saw that this one, who looked very angry, was one of his own pictures of the schoolmaster.

THE Schoolmaster

" This is the way you wasted your precious time. Look at ME. Don't you think I'm an object ? " cried another very badly scribbled drawing of a skeleton or ghost. " Now we're going to Haunt you—like Everything ! "

Saying this, they all began dancing around Johnnykin, and singing, while for music was heard a horrible tune of blows of switches, and the crying of boys being whipped.

The Ghost

"This is very dismal, and these creatures are very tiresome," thought Johnnykin. So he looked in his book. "I dare say," he continued, "there's some way laid down in it for getting rid of them?" So he read:

"Now this boy Johnnikin bethought himself to ask the Figures if they were not happy. For if they were not, there was in the House a greate Sponge wherewith to wipe them out."

"I say, you ungrateful noisy Wretches," cried Johnnykin, "havn't you led a happy life here since I drew you and rubbed you out?"

"First rate," said the robber. "Jolly as Sand-Boys. *Boo!*"

"But suppose I rub you out again," replied Johnnykin. "Where would you be then? Utterly gone for ever. And there's a great Sponge in the School-House and I see the Slate where you live. Here goes!"

All the figures at once turned as pale as chalk-marks, fell on their knees and began crying for mercy.

The robber dropped his weapons and exclaimed:

"Oh, forgive us! You did draw us—do not

withdraw us from life! Oh, don't wipe us out again. Listen to the Voice of Nature!"

"Yes—do listen to the Voice!" "Please listen to the Voice!" "Oblige us by directing your attention to the Voice!" cried all the Figures.

"Well," said Johnykin, "since you are polite, you may live. But what becomes of you all?"

"The first time anybody draws a Brigand with a lead pencil," said the robber, "I shall pass away from this slaty existence, and become myself a pencil-picture and a better man. I mean a better drawn one."

"But what becomes of the Lead-Pencil drawings?" asked Johnnykin, who thought this was very curious indeed.

"They go into the water-colour world, or etchings, and so on to oil-paintings and statues. We all keep going on for ever. Ah!" he cried, "I feel it—I *know* it! Somebody's drawing a Brigand *now* with a lead-pencil. Yes—as my last hour draws nigh, I know who it is.   It's a young lady in London.   She adores Brigands, and lives in Russell Square.   Every mark she makes draws me away.   My friends, farewell!   I shall no longer revel or slumber on the slate.   I am led hence!"

Johnnykin thought the Dying Brigand surrounded by the other sketches was a touching sight. But as soon as he had faded away, they all bowed farewell, and retreated into the slate. So Johnnykin walked on reading in his book and found this :—

"Now he came to a lone place among Rocks and Streams, hard by a great Wood.   There he lookt up from his Booke and saw a strange House like unto a Pumpkin.   This House did belong to a Man, of whom an old Song spake thus :—

"'Peter, Peter, Pumpkin-Eater
    Had a Wife and coulan't keep her ;
    He put her in a Pumpkin-Shell,
    And there he kept her very well.

" 'Peter, Peter, Pumpkin-Eater
Had another and didn't love her,
But Peter learned to read and spell,
And then he loved her very well.' "

Johnnykin looked up, and saw by the road-side a great round yellow thing, which had windows and a door. Over the door was the name

" PETER PUMPKIN-EATER, ESQ.,"

and on the step sat Peter, reading a book. Seeing Johnnykin he arose, and without so much as saying How do you do? began like a clergyman preaching :

" What a treasure, Sir, is learning ; and what would Life be without Letters ? I, Sir, was a brute once. I was so ignorant that I did not know how to build a house, and was obliged to put my first wife into this dwelling. Then I married another, but owing to my sad ignorance I hated her. One day, however, I found a spelling-book, and she persuaded me to learn only A B C, when

I fell madly in love with her, and have been so ever since. Now I can read all words of two syllables, and I possess every virtue. In fact, Sir, I am as good as any man can be; and I

believe that if I keep on as I have begun, I shall be the most intelligent and refined person in existence. You have passed, Sir, in this forest, a place where some effort was made to punish you for time wasted in school-hours. Owing to my love of letters, I have received the more agreeable appointment of rewarding youth for what it has done well—for the lessons learned and for general good behaviour. Oblige me by looking in that book which you carry, and by reading aloud the first sentence you see."

Johnnykin did as Peter requested and read :

" This Boy, Johnnikin, was always good and true. Therefore Peter did give him a first-class prize as a Rewarde of Merit."

" I am very glad," said Peter, " that I am able to give you a nice prize. You are the very first person who ever had the patience to listen to my account of myself. Wait a minute ! "

Saying this Peter went into his Pumpkin, and Johnnykin read in his book :—

" This man Peter had one Day found a great Treasure, when he was digging in the Forest. In itt was a fine Sword, whych had once belonged to an old Saxon king. And this Sword he gave to

Johnnikin, for verily he was the first Person who ever had patience to listen to Peter when he did talk of Himself."

Peter came out of the House with a very fine old sword, and said :

" I have been consulting with my wife, and she thinks as I do—and therefore very wisely—that a sword will be useful to you in this wild country. Accept the Reward of Merit ! "

Johnnykin thanked Peter very warmly, and went his way. The country became wilder and more desolate, the trees grew few and far between, and sometimes a strange feeling came over him, as if he were getting over the ground by miles in minutes, though he walked slowly, just as a man looking lazily at a vast country from a high mountain may take in a league at a glance, though he look ever so slowly. Then he began to read again, and saw these words :—

" And when it befel that the Boy Johnnikin had gone further on into this Land of the Gobblins, which some Men call the Land of Doubt, and was walking along the Way——"

Here Johnnykin heard a loud cry beneath his foot, "Don't tread on me!"

He looked, and saw it was a Great Snail.

"But the Book says nothing about *your* being here!" said Johnnykin, impatiently.

"Yes it does. Here's a picture of it. Don't

you see—a Boy treading on a Snail? Read on !"

"He trod on the Snail without knowing it, for he was so busy reading that he did not see her.

THE RUSH FAIRIES

Then He went on through a lonely, dreary Land, till he came to a little Streame which ran by, and in this Streame He saw naught save Rushes waving in the Wind, or as it seemed, dancing in the Water."

"It seems to me," said Johnnykin, as he looked at the Rushes more carefully, and saw the green leaves changing to pretty little faces, and white arms and hands, "that you look more like Water-Maids sporting in the brook than plants."

"We are both," said the tallest and fairest. "All of us Water-plants are alive and like fairies sometimes. I'm the Queen. Read on in your book, and, oh!—don't forget to turn your ring, Sir!"

So he read:

"Which were Fairies, such as dwell in Brooks or Fountains, far in lonelie Lands."

"You are not Witches, then?" asked Johnnykin.

The Queen laughed, and they all began to sing:—

> *"Let Witches tell*
> *Of evil spell,*
> *Though what they say be true,*

Yet list to me,
And ye shall see
What Fairy Girls can do.

" Oh ! the Rushes that grew in the bubbling stream
Did sing with the Birds at morning beam,
With a one—two—three !
How merry were we
When we saw the Foame dash over.

" Lone 'mid the rocks
Far hides the Fox,
No other may come near him,
On his back we sit,
Leap over the pit,
So little the Fairies fear him.

While the Rushes which grew in the bubbling stream
Did sing with the Birds at morning beam,
With a one—two—three !
How merry were we
When we saw the Foame dash over."

"Ladies !" said Johnnykin, "if you please !— "

"Look in your book," said the Queen, with a smile.

" Tell me whither I must go. And the Water-Fairies did all laugh aloude, which with the Murmur of the Streame made an excellent pleasant Noise—yea, a most sweet Musicke, for the Water did seem to him to sing, ' Marjolaine! Marjolaine!' as it ran away."

"Go straight on, Sir, any way you please," said the Queen of the Rushes. "What you seek you will find, soon enough. Good Knight—good night!"

And he read:

" The Fairy kist her Hand, and the Boy went his Way. Very sorry he was to see the last of these prettie little Water-Girlies. So he walked on, ever hearing as he went, the last words of the Maid's Song :—

> " ' Though Snowe be here,
>   And Winter drear,
>   I fear no Frost or Cold,
>   The Wood-Elf's arm
>   Doth keep me warm,
>   The whiles he singeth bold

H

"' How the Rushes that grew in the Bubbling Stream
Did sing with the Birdes at Morning Beam,
With a one—two—three!
How merrie were we
When we saw the Foame dash over.'"

Johnnykin could not help thinking how pleasant it would always be whenever he should sit
of a summer day by a stream, and see the flags
and rushes moving in the water, and hear them
rustling, to know that they were really little
living fairy maids. Soon he came into a broad
and weary place. Beyond it were sandy dunes,
and beyond this the sea. As the water rolled
in shore there came up from it little puffs or
small grey clouds, driven on land by the wind;
but, as he looked, these became knights and ladies
on horses, riding wildly about or capering madly
here and there. At one time a knight with his
lance would gallop at the others, and then they
would all fall like raging bears on one another.
And he saw in his book :

" The Boy did note one very strange Thing, and this was that their Horses seemed to bound like nothing on Earthe—yea, to almost fly like Birds, ever rising and falling."

" It is a curious party," said Johnnykin. " Those three riders who seem chief among them must be the Three Brethren out of Spain ! "

And as he said this, all the Knights rode upon him at once, as if they wished to bowl him over headlong. But Johnnykin stood quite calm and firm, and then, when the whole party came thundering down on him, drew his sword and dashed upon them. Just then he found he could bound and rise and skim along in the air too, and he did rise, to his great delight like a wild eagle, keeping above his foes and hitting at them below him. He became very angry and earnest, and they soon fled, sweeping and flying afar in great circles, like frightened wild-fowl.

" But they soon came, bounding merrilie up againe, wild and gay, all singing a prettie little old song :—

" ' *Hey diddle ding,*
I heard a Bird sing
Of a Knight that flew up to the moon,
Hey diddle day!
I heard a Bird say
That his Enemies fled away soon.' "

And now not a word was spoken, but Johnnykin and all went bounding along and away.
He could not help crying "Hurrah!" for in all
his life he had never felt so gay and glad. It
seemed to him to be no matter that they had
all been fighting, or that he had no horse, for
he now went flying as fast as any of them, and
so they went skying along, good friends and
well met. But as they fled far over forest and
hill in the clear moonlight, Johnnykin saw some
one approaching them. It was a wild young
Witch, with flowing hair, sailing with the wind
on her broomstick. And, coming by him, she
said:

"Johnnykin—why don't you ride your sword

as I do my broom ? You'll find it ever so much easier."

"Thank you," he replied. "Happy thought !

Ah ! how jolly—what a lark it is to fly like this by night over the world."

" And don't forget," said the Witch, " to turn
your ring.   There are only a few seconds left now."

Keeping by his side, the Witch made her
broom and his sword fly at a tremendous rate.
Then she snapped her fingers when the moon was
over-cast, and there flew from them, like a river,
thousands of sparks. And as the witch-fire flew
she sang :—

" *Violet darkle and rosemary ray,*
  Spinning, the sparkle goes rushing away!
  But my fingers are scarlet, and while they are bright,
  The road of the swan is a river of light,
  And while fire's in the flint or a light in the sea,
  While you ride on our road there'll be gleaming for
    thee.
  For the fire in the foam which I breathe when I swim,
  And the light in the stone which puts life in each
    limb,
  Shall all sparkle out for a glory to him!"

This was sung in a sweet, loud voice, and
Johnnykin thought the Witch very kind. Just
then he leaned forward, and as the light rayed
out very brightly, he cried in astonishment :

" Chesmé ! "

And Chesmé laughed so with him that she nearly fell off her broom and he from his sword.

" I say ! " cried Chesmé, to one of the knights —" do get this gentleman a horse ! "

" There's your chance," said the rider, pointing down to earth. Johnnykin looked and saw the Dark Tower again, and standing by it was a stately mounted knight with a lance.

Down dipped Johnnykin's sword like an intelligent creature, and in an instant he found himself almost falling on the knight, who attacked him with fury. But Johnnykin assailed him so that the other went rolling and bowling horse and man to the ground. Then Johnnykin catching the steed by the mane leaped lightly into the saddle, and as soon as he had done so, the other with as bold a jump seated himself behind him.

" Come, now ! " exclaimed Johnnykin—" this isn't fair. It's my horse now—the Book says so— see if it doesn't," he cried, producing his dear little volume.

"And the Book speaks the truth," said the Knight, throwing his arms round him, as the horse gave a start, to keep from falling. "Why it's *our* horse now, Johnnykin!"

There was a loud laugh over head from Chesmé, who made a splendid burst of fireworks at this instant, and Johnnykin turning his head, saw the helmet fall away, and the armour change to a lady's dress. And the face of the lady was all set in golden hair, and it was Marjolaine. Now the ride became merrier and wilder—hurrah! hurry! off and away they went, Johnnykin and Marjolaine with Chesmé on her broom, sometimes high in the air, sometimes near the ground, but always hallooing and jesting and frolicking. There was a grand old gentleman who seemed to lead, and Marjolaine said his name was Herne the Hunter.

All at once as they dashed by a covert they heard a terrible cry, like *Week! week! week!* and a great fierce creature rushed out of the bush. It appeared to be some kind of wild boar. In an instant Herne and all were after it full chase.

"Give me your sword! quick!" said Marjolaine
to Johnnykin. "There now, it's changed into a
boar-spear. Take it. Try to kill the swine if you
can!"

Johnnykin was delighted. He could see the
great creature dashing on in the moonlight, and
then vanishing in the shadow of the gorse, while
the others leaped over him, and galloping before,

turned him.   All at once Johnnykin found himself close by the beast.

"Now,   Johnnykin!—now—*now!*"   shouted Marjolaine.

Johnnykin drove his spear right at the pig. As he did so it gave a horrible squeal and burst asunder, falling into pieces.   But every piece as it fell and lay on the ground looked like a bit of broken earthenware, or a potsherd, while from the middle, as it broke up, poured a heap of money.

"It was a Money Pig," said Marjolaine.   "It must have escaped from the house of some Scotch farmer.   But take the money, Johnnykin; it is yours!"

A boy who was riding with them gathered the money and gave it to Johnnykin.

"There are just fifty-eight guineas, a half-crown, and a nine-pence."

"Be sure and breathe on the money!" said Marjolaine.   "What is that in your mouth?   A leaf?   Put it with the money!"

Johnnykin did so.

"Come," cried Chesmé—"read us a bit from your book, and let's hear what it has to say about you as a hunter."

So he read aloud these lines:

"Johnnikin, he did kill a prettie Pigg,
It was not very little, and it was not very bigg.
Marjolaine turning his sword to a spear,
Said, 'Ride the Boar down, quicke! never fear!'
Johnnikin did as Marjolaine said,
And in a minute the wild Pigg was dead.
The Pigg burst open, that was very funny,
Johnnikin found itt all full of money:
This is the Historie of them all three;
Marjolaine, Johnnikin, and the Money-Pig-gie."

They rode on, and Herne led them up a gradually rising ground. It grew steeper and steeper, until it became a flight of thousands of white marble steps, but the horses flew all the faster. All at once he found himself dismounted and alone—yes, in a second, and standing before

a great door, while Herne and all his party
bounded away high in the air. As they went
he cried after them, " Marjolaine ! Marjolaine ! "—
and he heard their voices, as if in echo, also crying
more and more faintly, " Marjolaine—Mar—jo—
laine ! "

" Thereupon He knockt at the Door, which
straightway was opened for him by the Gobblin."

THE GOBLIN MEETING

CHAPTER V.

THE GOBLIN MEETING—THE CHURCH MOUSE—LITTLE
BOY BLUE AND CHARLEY CAKE-AND-ALE WITH
HIS TRICKS AND JOKES—FAIRY FORTUNE-TELLING
—WILLIE WINKIE—THE ABSURD AND THEIR
SONGS—HOW OLD BOGEY WENT BACK TO THE
COAL-CELLAR.

 E found himself in
the old Church. But
it seemed to be many
times larger than
usual, and it was
swarming with thou-
sands of Goblins who
were all over the building. Some were on the

ground, and some swinging from webs like spiders,
and others buzzing, fluttering, and flying up in the
air like bees and birds and butterflies. Boughs
had grown out of the great pillars, and on these
many were perched like roosting fowls, clucking
and talking; while others had built nests, and
put up brackets in all kinds of places. It was
warm and comfortable, and there was a pleasant
delicate smell as of pine-boughs, roses, hot plum-
cake, pastilles, hyacinths, coffee, sherry wine,
lobster-salad, and eau de Cologne—which Johnnykin thought was very nice, because it smelt like
a party.

As he entered with the Goblin, they were
met by a small person with a pitiful pointed
face and a very long tail, who caught the Goblin
by the arm, and said:

"Do pray do something for me. I'm so *very*
poor. I should like to have what will be left
from supper. Don't you think they'd make a
Collection for me?"

"Is that the Sexton?" asked Johnnykin, after

the Goblin had promised the poor person to do something for him.

"Sexton!" replied his friend. "No; it's the

THE·CHURCH·MOUSE·

Church Mouse. Did you never hear of a man's being as poor as a Church Mouse? He is awfully poor, but that's because he's a poor creature in

I

every way. I don't believe if you gave him a Cheese for a conundrum he'd ever find his way into it."

"But a Cheese couldn't be a Conundrum, you know," said Johnnykin.

"What's the Moon made of?" asked the Goblin sharply.

"I have heard," said Johnnykin, "that a stupid person couldn't tell the Moon from a Green Cheese."

"Can you guess why they say so?" asked the Goblin.

"No," replied Johnnykin.

"Then that's a Conundrum because *you* can't guess it."

"That's all Nonsense, you know," replied Johnnykin, adding in his vexation:

> *"He who calls every lie a 'myth,'*
> *And every question a 'conundrum,'*
> *Might just as well call all men Smith,*
> *And beat all day on one drum."*

But before he could finish this reply, the Goblin vanished with a laugh, and he felt Somebody twitch his elbow.

It was a Boy—a very little Boy all in Blue, with blue shoes and cap, a little hunter's horn hung around his neck, and a little sheep by him.

I 2

"Well, my little man," asked Johnnykin, "who are you?"

"If you please, I'm Little Boy Blue," was the reply; "and the two young ladies sent me to say they'd like to speak to you."

Johnnykin looked up and saw Marjolaine beckoning to him from a corbel, or sort of old stone bracket at the top of a pillar, where she was nestling with Chesmé. They had bouquets and fans, and seemed very stylish indeed. Notwithstanding all his jumping and flying that night, Johnnykin could not think how to get up to them, till Marjolaine threw out a pink ribbon with a sugar-plum tied to the end. It unrolled downwards in a most wonderful manner until Johnnykin caught the sugar-plum, when in an instant he was drawn up through the air, and found himself seated very comfortably with them.

"There's a pretty fish to catch now!" said Chesmé, laughing, as they landed him. "How did you like your Story-book? And what a nice ride we had!" she added without stopping;

" and oh! do look! there goes that hateful
mean-spirited Church Mouse!—the wretch had
the impertinence just now to fall on his knees
before me, and beg me not to eat him. I told
him I had done for ever with all such horrid

vulgar creatures as mice and cats — and I
declare! — here comes Charley-Loves-Good-Cake-
and-Ale! How do you do, Charley?"

This was a very merry-looking youth, whom

Johnnykin at once remembered having seen among the wild riders in the wilderness.

"How do you do, my Lady?" he said to Marjolaine, and bowed to all. "A jolly good gallop you had," he added to Johnnykin, smiling. "A good horse, eh, that of yours? The Cock-Horse from Banbury Cross—none better."

"I am sure you seemed to be much better mounted," replied Johnnykin. "You rode on one horse and had another led all the time."

Charley Cake-and-Ale looked funnily at him, and said softly:

"Mum's the word. All a take-in. Goblin work, you know. The horse *I* rode was only Shank's Mare. She looks pretty well; but then you're always on your feet when you're riding, so that you might just as well be walking, you know."

"But then there was your other horse," said Johnnykin.

"Well—yes—but that was Hobson's Choice. You see I had the choice of Shank's Mare or

none. So I took Shank's Mare, and that gave
me Hobson's Choice also; but neither of them
is good for much unless you can do just as
well without. If you can, they answer very
well."

"I wonder," thought Johnnykin to himself,
"if there's anything real among these people."

Marjolaine caught his eye, and said with a
quiet smile:

"*I'm* real; that is, you will find me so by
and by. The play isn't over, and it will last a
long time yet. By and by you will find what
the reality is among us. There's always a new
life for Anybody who wills it."

"Good-bye!" said Charley. "I must be off.
I've got an appointment with Jumping Joan and
Handy Spandy——"

"Jack-a-Dandy," added Chesmé.

"Yes—there they are. Glad to have met
you," he said to Johnnykin. "We'll all meet
at supper. *Bon soir*, my Lady!" And off went
Master Charley singing a song—

" Let's rink and be merry,
And ride and rejoice;
Tho' on One Shilling sherry,
And Hobson his choice.
I'm a Goblin, I know,
So it's proper and fit
To be always a-gobblin'
Or tippling a bit."

"They say he used to be Charles the Second," said Marjolaine, "because he is so merry."

"I'm sure," said Chesmé, "that in anything like eating or drinking and flirting he must have been Charles the First and Second to Nobody. I asked him once if he had ever been Charles the Second, and he had the impudence to reply that he had never been concerned in a duel in his life. But he is jolly company, for he has so many tricks, yet never harms or teases anybody. I don't believe he ever went or came twice in the same way. Just look now and see him!"

Saying this, she lightly snapped her fingers. Johnnykin had observed the other Goblins doing

this when they wanted to call one to the other.
Charley was far across the Church in a nest like
theirs, with some very frolicsome friends, and
his back was towards them; but the instant the
fingers snapped, he turned round and made a
sign to Chesmé that he understood and was
coming. He held between his fingers an almond
sugar-plum, which began to swell into a large
egg, and making a sign to Chesmé to catch, he
threw it to her. As it left his fingers he disappeared; but as Chesmé caught the egg it broke,
and out of it jumped Master Charley, very small
indeed, but he at once shot up to his usual size.

"Here we are again!" he cried, "as large
as life——"

"And twice as un-natural," replied Chesmé.

"Why, Charley! what is that you have
hanging to your watch-chain?" asked Marjolaine.

It was a very pretty little gold cannon.

"I made that myself this afternoon," replied
Charley with pride. "And a hundred and fifty
more, all exactly like it."

"Indeed!" said Johnnykin, "and how?"

"Playing at billiards," answered Charley. "Other players let their cannons lie on the table.

Making a Cannon.

I picked mine up as fast as I made them, and put them aside. We were playing for guineas, so of course the cannons were gold."

"You must have very peculiar balls for such a game," remarked Johnnykin.

"So we have. In our Goblin game we have them very small. I always play with Peas."

"And what do you strike the Peas with?" asked Johnnykin.

"With the Cues of course. P's and Q's always go together. But then you must mind them, you know."

"I've seen very little fairy children play with peas," said Chesmé. "There's an old song about it. Listen!"

> "*Fairies play at marbles*
> *When the moon is bright,*
> *You may see them rolling,*
> *All the summer night.*
> *While round the hill,*
> *Tinkle! goes the rill.*

> "*When the wood is quiet,*
> *They blow the fairy horn;*
> *And with peas for marbles,*
> *They play among the corn.*
> *While round the hill*
> *Tinkle! goes the rill.*

"*When you find a pea-pod*
On the stem, all bare,
With the little marbles gone,
The fairies have been there
While round the hill
Tinkle! goes the rill."

"Peas," said Charley, "make very nice pudding for pork. By the way, that was a nice run we had after that Pig. But I had a hunt this morning which put me to my trumps, and never a pack ready. I was in the kitchen, when all at once a Rabbit jumped out of a hole in a

cheese. Fortunately, there was a Horse standing before the fire, so I mounted at once."

"A Horse in the kitchen!" said Johnnykin, "and before the fire!"

"Where else should it be?" replied Charley. "It was a Clothes Horse. So after the Rabbit I flew, with the Dogs at her heels!"

"Were your dogs there also?" asked Johnnykin.

"Certainly—the Fire-Dogs. One must do what one can at a pinch. And so, after a nice gallop, I got my game."

the Fire Dogs

"Wasn't a Cheese a queer place for a Rabbit to come out of?" asked Johnnykin.

"Not at all," replied Charley. "It was a Welsh Rabbit. They always come out of Cheeses."

"I should as soon think" replied Johnnykin, "of saying that butterflies come out of Butter."

Chesmé laughed. "Words are things" she said, "in Goblin-land. But wouldn't you like to know," she added, "how to tell fortunes by butterflies. I have got in my pocket a little old book of Fortune-Telling by a Gipsy Fairy. And this is what it says of

BUTTERFLY LUCK.

"If a butterfly sit on your hand,
  You'll be the luckiest in the land,

                              On Sunday.

"*If a butterfly sit on your head,*
  A handsome girl you're sure to wed,

                    On Monday.

"*If a butterfly sit on your arm,*
  No one will ever wish you harm,

                    On Sunday.

"*If a butterfly sit on your thumb,*
  Good luck is coming or soon to come,

                    On Monday.

"*If a butterfly sit on your wrist,*
  A pretty girl waits and wants to be kissed,

                    On Sunday.

"*If a butterfly touch you with its wing,*
  It's a sign you will have a diamond ring,

                    On Monday.

"*If a butterfly sit on your hat,*
  You'll have a gift and of gold at that,

                    On Sunday.

"*If a butterfly come in your hall,*
  Your friends will be great, your foes be small,

                    On Monday.

" But if you harm a butterfly,
    For that you'll suffer before you die,
                On Sunday or on Monday."

" Please read some more," said Johnnykin.
" Certainly.   Here is

" ' *THE FISH-FORTUNE.*

" ' *When you're by the river, if you see a fish*
    Jumping from the water you should make a wish;
    And if you can speak it before he's out of sight,
    The wish will all be granted that very day or night.'

" And here is a spell by which very good
children conjure the spirit of a star :—

K

"'THE STAR-CHARM.

"'*If you will take a looking-glass,*
And hold it to a star,
And look upon it at the light
Which comes from heaven afar;

" While you are looking in the glass,
If never a word you speak,
An angel will come down from heaven
And kiss you on the cheek.'

—only you can't see her, you know; but sometimes you can just feel it on your cheek like a little breeze. And then they say whenever you find a very perfect little pebble, that is a Fairy present. Listen!

" ' Down in the pond where fishes dive,
Are little green fairies all alive,
There they swim and there they creep,
Down in the water ever so deep.

" There never were people half so neat,
They scrub the rocks with hands and feet,
They polish the stones wherever they're found,
And that's what makes the pebbles so round.

" And when you walk by the water bright,
And find a pebble round and white,
You may see for yourself what fairies do,
Who placed it there as a present for you.' "

"Why are they so anxious to make presents to strangers?" asked Johnnykin.

"Because if they can only do anything for a real person, or for a higher being of any kind, or even so much as get noticed, the poor little things get on in the world a bit—or at least remain as high as they are. After a while, when they get to be beings that can walk on land, they're allowed once a year or so a little holiday to be like real people—and oh, how they do enjoy it! Hear what my Book says about

"'THE TOADS.

"'Over the forest and far away,
Where the hills are green and the rocks are grey,
There's a place which only the fairies know,
Where once a year the toads all go.

"'And there they are changed to ladies fair,
With great black eyes and curly hair;
And have fawn-skin dresses and silver rings,
And coral beads and beautiful things.

" ' There they dance and there they play,
Where the hills are green and the rocks are grey,
But it only lasts till there falls a rain,
And they all are turned into toads again.'

"If you will only repeat that poem to a Toad, you can have no idea how charmed the poor thing will be!"

Here a murmur was heard just outside and below their nest as of voices of children playing

merrily. They looked and saw Little Boy Blue
with several others, who had built or found a
projecting ledge on the pillar, where they were
busy at something which plainly gave them great
delight.

"Ah! there's Willie Winkie among them!"
said Chesmé. "He's my pet darling, and Little
Boy Blue is Marjolaine's. Come up, Willie!"

Saying this she reached over and hauled in
a darling little boy about three years old who
had nothing on but his night-gown. Johnnykin
thought he had never seen such a pretty little
fellow.

"Well, Willie!" said Chesmé, "what are you
little ones doing?"

"We've dot a gate piece of dough out of 'e
titchen," said Willie. "An' we've dot a gate
board, an' Tom Sum an' 'Ittle Boy Boo are cuttin'
'ittle 'cool tildren out on 'e board—'ittle boys and
dirls. And 'Ittle Miss Muffet makes 'em alive,
so 's 'ey can talk. And 'Ittle Bo-Peep has dot
a white wose an' she turns 'e wose-leaves into 'ittle

'cool-books an' pimers for 'e tildren, an' *my* tildren all know their letters a'ready as far as F.——"

"But why do you keep them all on the Board?" asked Johnnykin.

Little Willie looked up with a droll glance.

"Dat's our 'Cool Board. If we didn't have a 'Cool Board 'e tildren wouldn't mind their lessons—pease let me go!"

And saying this Willie slid out of Chesmé's lap and slipped over the edge and in an instant was heard shouting gaily to his little two-inch pupils, who were very restless, because Willie had given them figs and cakes to sit on and these they kept slyly eating, notwithstanding his reproofs.

"How pretty Willie is," said Johnnykin. "It will be a pity when he grows up."

"He'll never grow up," said Marjolaine. "He is the oldest of all the Goblins, for he is the Spirit of Baby Talk, and Baby Talk you know came before Fairy Tales."

Far away, down on the floor, Johnnykin saw, seated in a ring a party of dim white creatures, like clouds, and without fixed shapes, yet each of them kept moving or rolling and curling all the while in such a way that in looking at it you saw or thought you saw a face or features changing into new ones, and its body or limbs passing into new forms. It was like looking at a figured curtain when the wind is blowing and one is half-asleep, and fancying one sees in its lines or flowers or folds

or stains something like pictures and profiles. With
Marjolaine's opera-glass he could see them very
plainly as they sat on the ground like a party
of Arabs in an encampment, and at last he began

THE FIGURE

to observe that just as other people in talking
move their features and make gestures, so these
wonderful cloudy things changed their entire faces
and bodies to express their thoughts. Their talk

was like telling a story with puppets but without speaking. But all was so quickly done that it tired him to look at them.

"Who are they?" he inquired.

"They—oh, they're the Absurd. Nobody knows anything about them. They're beyond Everything and Everybody. They sit there singing among themselves all the time, but nobody knows what."

"I do," said Charley. "I overheard some of their song once. It's as deep as a Devonshire lane and about as muddy. They call it the Poetry of the Future. This is a verse of it :—

> "*Softly the Vampire*
> *Sung to the Snail,*
> '*You caught the Nightmare,*
> *I held her tail.*
> *But while the Beetle*
> *Crowed on the Post,*
> *Deep in the Greybeard*
> *I drowned the Ghost.'*"

"That's horrid nonsense, you know," said Chesmé; "but I'm sure it would be a great deal more horrid if the awful things were to explain it!"

Just as she said this there came a soft swell of music and the voices of the Absurd were distinctly heard.

> " *Greenly the Wildfire*
> *Opened his eyes,*
> *Sang to the Corpse-light,*
> ' *Come, bake the pies !*
> *Heed not the Ghoul, love !*
> *Trust not his smile,*
> *Out of the Mosque, love,*
> *He stole the tile.'* "

And then a mysterious Voice, which sounded as if the singer were nothing but a Voice, made of melody and misery, sang—

> " *There's a red cloud on the Mountain which I know—*
> *but He !—*
> *There are Shadows in the Fountain which You know—*
> *but She !—*
> *In the Palm*
> *Rose the Psalm*
> *Of the wandering Banjaree.*

" There are gold shells on the strand
We may gather—but They !—
There's a bark beside the sand
While you are at your play
In the Cavern
By the Tavern
With the Starlight far away.

" And the Waves are rolling on in the Moonlight—but Ye !
Await the purple dawn from the Islands—while we
By the River
Sit and quiver
At the lonely Romanee."

"Good-bye!" said Charley. "That's enough
for me. I'm off!"

This time Charley turned himself into a great Frog and made a clear leap across the church. Now if he had done what he intended he would have alighted full on the face of Margery Daw who was waiting for him. But as she saw him coming she held out her fan at him, and as she

did so it changed into a great, cruel-looking carving-fork. But Charley was too quick for her with his goblin magic, for as she held the fork out, it turned into a twig, the prongs shot out into branches, and became a pretty bough full of leaves and flowers, among which Master Charley fell without any

harm. But it also made very little impression, for an instant after they saw him change into a bottle of Champagne and shoot himself with a tremendous *pop!* as the cork — the bottle vanishing — into a distant place whence he immediately returned as a sky-rocket, knocking his three friends this time head over heels, whereupon they set upon him and beat him, and there was a terrible fight, which was, apparently very much in earnest.

It was however, speedily stopped by a hideous creature with a great stick. He was black, hairy, and awfully ugly, and at one look from his dreadful eyes Master Charley and his companions became quiet as mice.

"Who is that?" asked Johnnykin.

"Bogey," replied Chesmé. "I believe he's one of the Absurd creatures. We don't see him often now-a-days. He can't really do anything you know—only frighten people. If you don't *believe* in him he isn't anywhere, though they say he lives in the Coal-Cellar."

Just as she said this Old Bogey rose up before them in all his terrors and glared at Chesmé, opening his great red mouth as if to swallow her alive, and crying *Boo!* Johnnykin shivered, but Chesmé only laughed and snapped a sugar-plum into his open jaws which were bigger and uglier than those of a hippopotamus. With a hideous grimace and a frightful roar of anger, Bogey sank down out of sight and disappeared in the floor.

"Tell me one thing more," asked Johnnykin.
"Who is Little Boy Blue? Is *he* old?"

"Yes," replied Marjolaine. "Wherever there

are blue eyes and blue skies in dear old England,
and while the blue sea surrounds it, and while

there are hay-fields, and while people think with love of the quiet days of the olden time, and while fairy tales are written for children—there will be Little Boy Blue."

As she said this Johnnykin looked into *her* blue eyes and saw in them the same sweet innocent look as in the little boy's and felt that she was to him what the Little Boy Blue is to all children "in summer when the days are long."

CHAPTER VI.

THE DREADFUL STUPIDS—THE GOBLIN REPORTS ON MISCHIEF—THE COMMITTEES ON ORANGE-PEEL AND TIP-CATS—THE FLYING OYSTERS AND TALKING PICTURES—MR. MANNERS.

an-tara-tar-an-ta-a-ta! went a loud trumpet. Then there was prompt silence, disturbed only here and there by the last frolicking of the wilder goblins or by the quieter ones settling down into places.

Tan-tara-tar-a-ta! blew the trumpet, more impatiently.

Then a procession came through the side door. The first part of it consisted of a great many gentlemen, mostly young. They all wore evening dress in a very evening manner, and had their hair parted in the middle, and bore small, neat mustachios. They were all very much alike indeed, and very solemn; and nearly all had eye-glasses, and stared through them at everybody, as if thinking, "Well!—what is it?—what do you want?" As they walked round and round, Johnnykin heard the spectators say with delight:

"How stupid!—how very stupid!—how dull. Isn't it wearisome? How tiresome! Parrots! And how real!"

"Those," said Marjolaine to Johnnykin, "are the Dreadful Stupids."

"What *is* the use of looking at them?" he replied.

"Don't you understand? When you Real people amuse yourselves you like to see queer merry folk like Goblins to make you laugh. We like to see stupid figures like common real people to make us dull. It calms one's mind so."

After the poor, young, Dreadful Stupids had marched a great many times about the church, they were followed by a party of ladies and gentlemen of all ages. The elderly and middle-aged dames were over-dressed, the young ladies stared very much like frogs, and all looked as if they had better have staid at home.

"Those," said Marjolaine, "are the People One Can't Remember for One's Life. And they are the greatest troubles in it. People, for instance, that one goes down to dinner with for the first time, and who can't talk a word. They are followed by the men and women who always remember you when you can't recall them. It's generally years after you've seen them for a second somewhere."

"And you like looking at this?"

"Certainly, we think it's charming — it's so very dull, and bores one so. It almost makes me feel sleepy. You know," she added, "that we never sleep in Goblin Land."

"Ah!" said Johnnykin, "*now* I can understand it all. You refresh yourselves with Stupidity, just as we do with sleep!"

"Yes."

"Then I think you would find mortal life very nice," replied Johnnykin.

The girls gave a deep, sad sigh, and looked at him as if they wanted him to say more. But he was quiet, and then they sighed again.

Tan-tara-ta-a! went the trumpet.

A very queer little Goblin now mounted the pulpit.

"That's Nick of Lincoln," said Marjolaine.

"Friends all, great and small," cried Nick, " I am glad to see you together again. As we have a great deal to eat, and drink, and talk, and laugh, by and by, we will proceed at once to business. The Committees on Mischief are first in order. Will the Chairman of the Committee on Orange-Peels please to report?"

A very mischievous lemon-faced monkey-looking Goblin here arose and said:

"The Committee have to report that in England alone during the past year, twenty-five thousand and ninety-eight people slipped on bits of orange-peel."

"*Hear! hear!*" cried all the party in Charley Cake-and-Ale's box.

"Four thousand one hundred and thirty of these people were hurt.

"Three hundred were seriously injured.

"The Committee have found that all of these sufferers declared it was a Shame, and that who-ever threw Peels about ought to be Severely Punished.

"They have also found that of all the people thus injured, there was not one who had not at some time in his or her life, carelessly flung orange-peel on pavements.

"The Committee on Orange Peels are of the opinion that Such is Life, and that if you are Virtuous you will be Happy, and Exchange is no Robbery."

There was immense cheering at this, the reason being as Chesmé explained that the remarks  in the concluding sentence were not only entirely new to everybody present, but that they sounded so much like the talk of real people that everybody was quite charmed. The trumpets blew *tara-an-ta!* and another sprite jumped up who announced himself as Chairman of the Committee on Puttings Things on Railroads.

"I have on record," he said, "eleven hundred cases of bad boys who put sticks and things on railroads or who threw stones at trains.

"All of these boys were constantly familiar with cruelty, harshness, and strife, and of course

were always thinking how they could do something desperate and cruel themselves.

"The Committee is of the opinion that those
who show the Cat the Way to the Dairy will
Bake as they Brew and by sowing the Wind
will reap the Whirlwind."

The cheers and trumpeting which followed this
Report having ceased, there was heard a tremendous
Mee-a-ow-ouh! and a creature like a frightful Cat
bounded on the pulpit. I am sorry to say that
Chesmé the instant she heard this uttered a loud
mee-ee-ow! in answer, and then, very much ashamed,
blushed up to her hair and hid her face in her
handkerchief, while Marjolaine appeared to be
almost angry and said,

"My dear—you surely forget yourself."

Of course Charley Cake-and-Ale hearing poor
Chesmé's cry set up an awful *mee-ow* opposite, in
which Margery Daw and all her select party
joined, until the entire house was in an uproar.
And then of course they began to scream Silence!
and Shame!

"I am so ashamed of myself," sobbed Chesmé ; "but I've only just left off being a cat."

"And I like cats *ever* so much," said Johnnykin, earnestly, "and you do mee-ow so sweetly."

When Chesmé heard this she dried her tears and said,

"I can't help it—it runs in the family. Once in Athens my dear Mamma forgot herself in the same way. She had been a Cat, but Venus changed her to a Young Lady——"

"Oh, I know that story," said Johnnykin. "It's down in Æsop."

"Is it really printed in a real book?" exclaimed Chesmé. "Oh, what a comfort! How happy I am! Our Family is known in the Real World! Do you hear *that*, Marjolaine?" Saying this Chesmé held up her head with great pride, and fanned herself, and looked as if she wished that everybody in the church knew what Johnnykin had just told her.

The Cat which was now in the pulpit had a

very singular shape. It was pointed
at both ends, and explained itself by
saying—

"I appear as Chairman of the Committee on Tip-Cats. We find that of late
the practice of Tip-Catting has greatly
increased, especially in London. Eleven
people have lost eyes, four hundred and
twenty-eight have been hit on the nose,
eleven hundred windows broken, and two
little boys have been taken up by the
Police and fined half-a-crown each. *Mee-ow!*"

"Come now, Johnny-
kin! You've had enough
of the committees, I
know—and I don't be-
lieve you think enough
of them is as good as
a feast."

"Therefore let's go to
supper!" cried a saucy
small voice, which came

from Chesmé's Silver Perfume bottle. Johnnykin looked and saw it sitting up on the edge
of the box, looking as pert as you please.

Flying to Supper

Before Johnnykin knew where he was, the
two young ladies had joined their hands, put
a shawl over them, and caught him up so that

he found himself sailing between them with inter-
locking arms high in the air. Down they came—
not very quickly, for I think they all liked the
fun of sailing about. Johnnykin observed that
all their " things"—that is the perfume bottle,
fans, and shawls, either put on wings or else
spread themselves and came flying after them.

They went down stairs, for the supper was
in the Crypt under the Church. And as they
entered, the splendour of the scene startled
Johnnykin. He had been looking at wonders
for hours, but this was the best of all. All round
the room was scenery like a diorama; far in the
distance, appearing entirely real, rose in gold or
crimson light, cliffs and castles, with towers and
turrets, pinnacles, precipices, ancient cathedrals,
strange-peaked houses, wild rocks, walls, stairs,
and great trees. All seemed far away, as far in
the olden time as in the distance. Beyond all,
here and there, was the Sea, and further still
in the blue were little rosy islands, and on these
again were little towers and towns. Johnnykin

could see on them broad white marble steps which went down into the green water, and with Marjolaine's glass perceived great vases with flowers on the steps and beautiful boats with high prows coming and going into the sun-set.

Nearer, but still far away, were hundreds of fine old gabled houses, with great porches, and vine-covered balconies, held up by odd monsters, high roofs, full of carving on the pointed fronts, and bow-windows supported by strange figures. Around them lay beautiful gardens, and all was as hushed and dreamy as in old times.   For the gardens were so quiet and the streets so still that it seemed as if it must be always Sunday and always summer there.   But there were people moving in it all, and, indeed, some-times the company in the supper-room wandered away into the town.   Then very far in the background, in the country, Johnnykin saw the Dark Tower, half asleep.   Out of the window came a very tiny figure which went along the road which Johnnykin had travelled.

He told this to Marjolaine who only said—
"Why didn't you tell me before? See here!"

Saying this she screwed up the glass, and
when he looked again he could see the little
man very plainly though miles away. It was
Friar Bacon. He walked on, disappearing sometimes among the trees or rocks, and then re-
appearing. Then he came to the Pumpkin House.
Johnnykin saw him talking to Peter while Peter
made a sign as of a sword.

All this time Johnnykin and the young ladies
were sitting comfortably at a table, while Little
Boy Blue was waiting on them.

He saw the Five Finger Brothers and the
Land of Doubt and the Brook with a little bridge
by which the Rushes sang and the sandy dunes
and the sea.

"Can you see the place where you killed the
awful Money Pig?" asked Marjolaine, suddenly.

He could, and also saw Friar Bacon come on
and grow bigger as he got nearer, until at last
he came into town, and then into the hall,

and after that to their table, where all greeted him.

"Hey, Blue, my Boy!" he cried, "a quart of

bitter ale! Well, Mortal Boy," he said kindly to Johnnykin, "so you got a sword out of Peter! Anybody that could listen to Peter talking about

M

himself deserved it. I wish when you go to London you'd take that sword to the British Museum and ask Mr. Franks if it isn't the original Excalibar of King Arthur. *He'll* know.

EXCALIBR

"He talks as if I were a man grown and going to London," thought Johnnykin.

Marjolaine smiled.

The supper room was splendid. There were flowers everywhere, a great many flying about in the air and coming to people to be taken. And there was such a wealth of gold and silver candelabras, vases, fountains, plate, and goblets, such gorgeous draperies, and such wonderful chairs and lounges, as all the palaces in the world could never show.

"You may call for Anything you like," said Friar Bacon as he sat down after dipping his hands in a gold ewer and drying them on a lace-edged napkin. "And if you want to eat for ever without its hurting you, just take a sip of the cordial in the bottle before you. That's my invention, Mortal Boy," he added, "and a good one, though I say it. The old monks all used it—jolly boys!"

"We always begin at Goblin parties by pulling crackers," said Chesmé. "Pull one with me!"

Johnnykin picked up a fine large cracker and they pulled. It went off with a horrible explosion, like a keg of gunpowder. Nobody was hurt,

but out of the blaze dropped something alive.
In a few seconds it grew to human size and
proved to be Master Charley Cake-and-Ale, as
lively as ever.

"Here we are again!" said Charley. "I
told you I'd be here. That's in History. Did
your Reverence say Oysters?" he suddenly asked
Friar Bacon, who smiled. "It was like your
wisdom. *I'll* give the order." Saying this Charley

picked up one out of a great pack of blank cards which were on the table in a silver cup, and wrote on it "Oysters for Five!" The card at once put

on Dragon-fly wings and departed, returning in a minute followed by a long train of Natives with some Lemons, who politely deposited themselves by the plates.

"Oysters are really getting dear," said Friar Bacon, after he had eaten six dozen. There was in fact quite a constant procession through the air of oysters flying to his plate on one side, and of shells flying away on the other. "I've seen the time, Mortal Boy, when you could get no end of them for what they now ask for one oyster. However," he added more cheerfully, "just wait till I perfect my great invention for

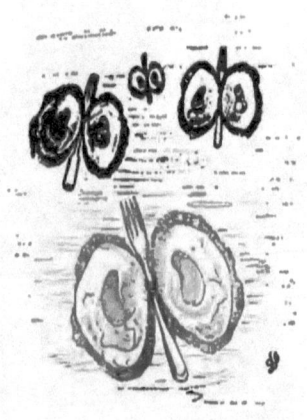

growing oysters by electricity, and then you'll see the good old Saxon prices again. I've made them grow so fast," said the Friar, "that they couldn't sleep—it kept 'em moving so!"

"Oh, look what I've found!" cried Charley Cake-and-Ale who had meanwhile, urged by his usual restlessness, gone forth on one of his little

excursions. He showed them Johnnykin's portfolio which had been left lying on the tomb in
the churchyard.

"It's mine," said Johnnykin.

"Prove it," said Charley.

"Speak!" said Chesmé to the Portfolio.

"Conjure it to speak," she added, impatiently
to the Friar.

"*Portfolius conjurissimus hockleybendibus
onus probandi!*" said the Friar solemnly to it.

The Portfolio at once jumped up on a pair
of long grasshopper legs and began to dance.

"Whose are you?" asked Chesmé.

The Portfolio performed several steps of a hornpipe, pointed a long grasshopper arm and claw at Johnnykin, and said, winking:

"*His'n.*"

"Good Saxon at any rate," said the Friar.

"May we see your pictures?" asked Marjolaine.

Johnnykin quietly opened his portfolio, saying nothing about his being "ashamed" of his drawings, or that they were "very poor." The first picture they saw was his portrait of the Goblin.

"Why, it's life itself!" said Chesmé.

"It wants expression," said Master Charley.

The picture rolled its eyes, and said in great anger—"I *don't*. Much *you* know about pictures, you Charley Cake-and-Ale—you Goblin Snob!"

Saying this, it became very highly coloured, and so animated in expression, that it jumped out of the paper, and growing up to life size in a second, sat down in a chair.

"Oysters?" asked Charley.

"Yes." And while he ate they looked at the sketches. All of them, even the merest scraps of figures, became alive as soon as anything

THE DRAWINGS ESCAPING

was said about them, and jumped out and ran away like cats and spiders, some hopping from the front and some vanishing through the back of the paper.

"They disappear, Mortal Boy," said the Friar,

"because you have not Fixed them. Be sure and remind me to give you a bottle of my patent fluid for fixing everything. It fixes drawings, poems, ideas, the mind or the eye, or the attention on anything. The kind sold in two shilling bottles will fix the heart and the affections for ever. But it has been very much improved by the Americans," added the Friar, with a sigh; "for I have heard that they profess to be able to put Anybody into an Eternal Fix, and I think it must be by some application of my invention. And now for the rest of supper. You, Charley, fly round and wait on the ladies! Mortal Boy— just taste that salmon. It's fresh as ever, though it was caught and cooked by the giant Finn Macoul once, a thousand years ago. Whoever tastes it will understand all the birds say all his life. When you're a great poet, as you will be some day, you'll thank me for telling you to eat it."

"Who is that gentlemanly person," asked Johnnykin, "whom I see all about the hall, here and there, standing behind people as they eat? He has been watching us several times."

"That!" said Chesmé; "oh— that's Manners! Mr. Manners you know! Some people always leave something on their plates for Manners, and that's how he gets his living. But he doesn't fare as well as he used to, since now-a-days people are not so particular about leaving anything for him."

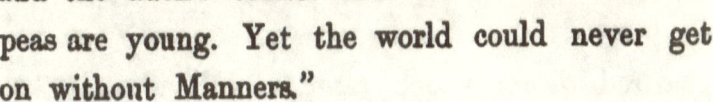

"Not much from me," said the Friar, "when I'm hungry, and the duck's tender and the peas are young. Yet the world could never get on without Manners."

"What makes him look so pale?" asked Johnnykin.

"Oh, it's because he eats such a dreadful mixture of things, and only such a little bit of each.

There are only little bits left for Manners, you know," said Chesmé. "Yet he ought to flourish; for I'm sure we should all be poor wretches if we grew up without Manners."

She had hardly spoken, when Johnnykin saw afar in the distant sky among the mountains

a red gleam which came rapidly along. As it approached, there came with it a roaring sound like that of a tempest; and in the strange light he could perceive something like a Giant, but a royal one, with an immense beard to which a Boy was clinging, and in which he was often hidden as they flew. Without stopping, the Two swept in their red storm-cloud over the Goblins, who gave the Giant three tremendous cheers, to which he and the Boy replied as they passed. It was a grand sight, though terrible; but the Goblins seemed much delighted, for they applauded till the last sound of the storm had died away.

"That," said Marjolaine, "is King Orian—one of the greatest in our Goblin world."

"And who is he?"

"That I can hardly tell you. Some think he is the Storm, some Speed. But whatever is fast and wild is his. That is all I know of him, except an old song which Friar Bacon can sing."

Here Charley took up a silver spoon, which he at once changed to a lute, and played with great skill while the Friar sang the song of

KING ORIAN.

" On a roaring wild bull King Orian rides,
    And spurs with a dagger his tawny sides;
    The wild North Wind is his friend so true,
    And over the mountain King Orian flew.

" He rode to the east and he rode to the west,
    Till he found a boy in an eagle's nest ;
    And over the water and over the foam,
    King Orian rode with the wild boy home.

" King Orian lives in the sunset red,
    And the lightning's sheet is his royal bed ;
    Into his long beard the wild boy crept,
    And safely the King and the wild boy slept.

" A falling star is King Orian's sword,
    And deep in the mountain his gold is stored ;
    And when night comes on and the clouds go by,
    He roars with the boy on the mountain high.

" So listen, my children, when winter comes,
    And hear in the tempest King Orian's drums ;
    For when storm and billows are beating high,
    The King and his wild boy are riding by."

CHAPTER VII.

FRIAR BACON AND THE CUP OF KING DJEM-SCHID—
THE FAIRY HARP OF HOP-O'-MY-THUMB—THE
HORN OF BALDER—THE TWO GIRLS BECOME
REAL PEOPLE WITH THE GOBLIN AND OWL.

S the supper went on, Johnnykin became happier every
minute. Whatever he want-
ed came flying whenever a
card was sent for it.
These cards were the most
obliging creatures. Some of
them insisted on getting
out of the silver cup and coming to the
guests, falling before them on their knees, and

clasping their little hands as if imploring to
be sent for Something. The Friar sent one
for a cup, and it came. It was of gold, and
set with gems; the outside shone like a looking-

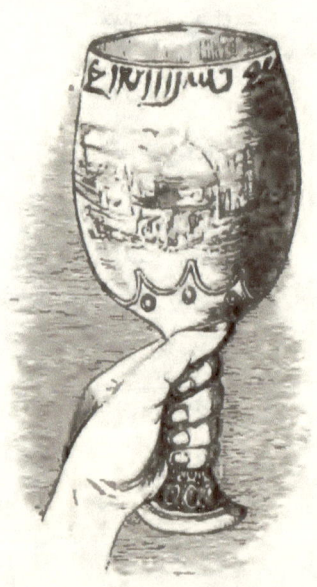

glass. And the Friar showed Johnnykin that
by looking at it carefully one could see as in
a mirror all that was passing in the world.
Cities, rivers, France, Italy, and everything
in all countries became large when they looked
at the particular place for a few seconds.

"This is the jewelled cup of the Persian king Djem-schid," said Friar Bacon. "To drink from it gives knowledge. Let us drink! all of us. And now for some good old Fairy music! Ah, Mortal Boy—a happy thought! I will send for the harp which Hop-o'-my-Thumb took from the Ogre!"

So off went a card messenger. With Marjolaine's opera-glass Johnnykin saw it flying for leagues in the distance over the sea, and finally disappear in the blue mountains. By and by something large and winged rose in the same place. It came flying like an eagle till it rested by them. It was the winged harp. On it sat a very small but fierce hero. This was the great Hop-o'-my-Thumb, whom Chesmé and Marjolaine at once seized, and began petting and feeding.

The Friar spoke to the Harp in Old Welsh, and told it to play his favourite tune. And then the Friar sang—

N

" *Oh, Brook ! why are you running*
  So fast to yonder plain ?
Oh, Mist ! why are you rising
  Up to the clouds again ?

" *Oh, Boy ! why are you going*
  Still up to seek a dream ?
Oh, Maid ! why are you flowing
  Still downward like the stream ?"

" *She's weary of her cloud-life,*
  He's weary of the plain :
Then let them meet and mingle,
  And fall to earth in rain.

" *In many a flower blowing,*
  In many a rainbow sweet,
In leaves and grasses growing,
  We'll see why they should meet."

The Northern Light played finely in Marjolaine's cheeks as the Friar ended this song,
and Chesmé took her hand and Johnnykin's.

But the Friar turned to Little Boy Blue and asked for his horn. Closing its smaller end, he turned it up, when something foamed over the edge.

"It's mead," said the Friar; "and this was once the horn of Balder. Drink away, my Mortal Boy — drink deep, and become an Immortal! for whoever tastes this becomes a Poet."

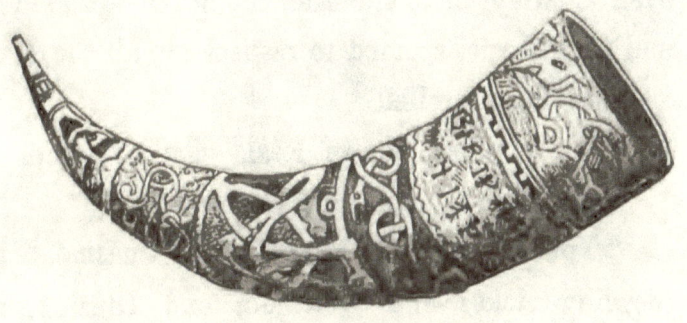

"Drink!" said the Goblin.

"Drink!" said Chesmé.

Marjolaine said nothing, but looked at him as he put the horn to his lips. It was like wine, and fire, and life, and honey, and light

and foam, and perfume, and everything delicious;
and as he drank the sound of the harp rang
and rilled as sweet as the Mead.

"One more pull, Mortal Boy. That's for a
drama.   One more—that's for a volume of
Ballads. Now a tremendous one. That'll be an
Epic. Pull away! Hurrah!"

"Why are you all so kind to me?" said
Johnnykin to Marjolaine. "So very kind! Why
even Charley Cake-and-Ale, though he quizzed me
and chaffed me, seemed to respect me all the time."

The Friar smiled.

"It's because you're Real," said Chesmé.

"And kind," said Marjolaine.

"You hav'n't got Magic," said Chesmé, "and
juggling-tricks, and Delusion, and Illusion, and
Confusion, or quick wit and a glib tongue. But
when I wanted the riddle, you found it for
me—which Charley could never have done. For
any *real* use, you——"

Here Marjolaine stopped Chesmé with a
glance.

But the deep draught of mead which had made him a poet, and all he had seen that night, had made Johnnykin very intelligent and bold.

"I remember," he said to Chesmé, "that you were very glad to leave the condition in which you changed from one animal to another, and to become a Goblin-girl all the time. But I thought that witches liked to be cats."

"Witches are low and vulgar things," said Chesmé; "though it certainly is a great lark to go off on a broom by moonlight. But I would not have done it for the world, only once in a way to please you. I'm of witch stock, but I hate it, and all our family have done their best to get above it."

"Well, as you like everything that is Real so much, I should think you'd like to be a Mortal Girl!"

As Johnnykin said this, the two girls looked at him very anxiously. Their faces became pale, and all the fire of their fairy nature was in their eyes.

"What shall I say when a Mortal speaks so to me?" said Chesmé, looking at the Friar. "What is the Goblin law?"

"You can only answer *direct* questions," replied the Friar. "But whatever a Mortal asks a Goblin must be honestly answered."

"Perhaps," said Johnnykin, "it is not polite in me to ask such questions."

But as he said this, he saw a sad, despairing look in Marjolaine's face.

"It is not much more impolite," said the Friar, "to put indirect questions in the form of remarks, though everybody does it. Put your questions directly, and they will be gladly answered—yes, very gladly indeed!"

Johnnykin noticed that Chesmé was looking at him, as if in great fear and anxiety.

"Would you like," he said, "to be a *real* girl?"

And with her whole soul she answered, "Yes."

"And you, too?" he asked Marjolaine.

And she answered, "Yes," as if wild with joy.

"How can it be done?" he continued.

And Marjolaine replied: "When a Mortal asks a Goblin to go with him into life—to marry him, or to be his friend, to join him, or aid and serve him in any way, and to be true to him for ever—and if he really means it, and deeply desires it, then the Goblin can go with him and become real."

"Would you like to go?"

Marjolaine smiled like an angel, and said, "Yes."

"Then come with me into life!"

He put his hand in hers, and then spoke to Chesmé.

"Will you come?" he asked.

"I will. Now I'm *quite* real!" she exclaimed, with pride and joy. "But I'm afraid there'll always be something of the Pussycat and Witch and Gipsy left about me, just as there will always be something of the Angel on the Monument about my Lady Marjolaine."

"There will always be something of the Goose left about you, Chesmé, dear," said Marjolaine.

"Will you come with your Owl?" asked Johnnykin of the Goblin.

"My Boy—with joy—to look after you young people. You'll need me!"

"And you?" he said to the Friar.

"Yes," replied the good man, "I'll join the party. I want to take a look at mankind again as One of Them. I've got several very fine inventions which would greatly benefit the world."

Chesmé and Marjolaine were weeping for joy in each other's arms, while the Fairy Harp was pealing and ringing, and the air was filled with perfume, and soft voices and sweet farewells were heard all around. Winged forms with lovely faces, quaint droll Goblins and merry Fairies came to bid good-bye; but as it grew sweeter and more musical, it also became dimmer, until all that Johnnykin knew was that the sturdy English arms of true old Friar Bacon were gently holding him as he sank to sleep. Yet he marked one thing—the beautiful round face of Little Willie Winkie, who came running up to Marjolaine, and said, taking her hand:

"Dood-bye! But oo'l see me 'dain one zese days where oo're a goin'. Dood-bye!"

And then lights, and Fairies, and Goblins, and flowers, and music, and voices, all faded away together.

CHAPTER VIII.

T was a bright summer morning, when Johnnykin awoke, and found himself lying by the old tomb, where he had sat the evening before. He looked up for the Goblin.

It was gone !

"It seems to me," said Johnnykin, "as if I had been seeing wonderful and beautiful things—but I can hardly remember them. I suppose it was all a dream."

His next thought was, that he felt stronger
than he had ever been, and then he observed
that his clothes were changed. He now had
on a handsome grey walking suit. By him lay

an overcoat, neatly strapped, his portfolio, and a
nice knapsack. He opened the latter. It contained linen and a dressing-case. In the case
was a mirror, and Johnnykin was startled as he
looked in it, to see a strange face. But, on

examining it carefully, he found that it was himself, but grown much older. If you had seen him, you would have added, "and much handsomer."

"And I am taller and larger," said Johnnykin. Then he looked in his pockets. "It's like robbing Somebody Else," he thought. He found a large purse, and in it fifty-eight guineas, a half-crown, and a nine-pence—all very old money—and with them a slightly-bitten leaf. This reminded him that he had heard if any one, when he finds fairy money, puts with it anything he may have in his mouth, it will remain his own. There was also a little, very old blank book, with silver clasps.

He thought for a minute over all these wonderful things, and then said, "Well—whatever has happened, I'm certainly better off. Somebody must be my friend to have given me all this!"

He arose, took his pack, and coat, and portfolio, and a stout cane, which he found with them, and walked through the Churchyard, and

along the lane, and across the Common. He saw
people that he knew, but all seemed to be five
or six years older, and there were a great many
children whom he did not know at all.

He went into his Uncle's house. There sat
the old man, very little changed. He did not
remember Johnnykin, but spoke to him civilly.
He thought he was an artist on a foot-journey,
who wanted to rest.

"Good day, Sir!" he said. "A painter, I
suppose. A good enough business, I dare say,
for some folks, but I never want any of mine to
try it. I've got a nephew, Sir, that once had a
turn that way. It's a queer story," said the old
man, "and you wouldn't believe it."

"Let me hear it," said Johnnykin.

"Well, Sir, that boy used to vex me out of
my life. He had no natural sense, and could do
nothing but draw pictures and talk in poetry.
It was a disease like, and he couldn't help it.
He got those unnatural fancies from his parents.
But he a'most drove me mad, and one day I'd

made up my mind to turn him adrift or bind him out to anything — I couldn't stand him any longer. But what do you think? That very evening he came in, and in five minutes I saw that a great change for the better had come over him. He sat down by the fire, and began to talk about horses and donkeys as nat'ral as if he'd been a groom. And from that day he stopped all his nonsense, and became the most sensible boy in the whole country-side. Ah! he's the comfort of my old age now—that's what he is! And here he comes!"

And in came the beloved Nephew. He said very little to Johnnykin, until the Uncle left the room, when he winked with a droll look, and said:

"See here. This is better for both of us. It's all as right for you as for me."

"So I hope," replied Johnnykin, "but I feel quite lost and puzzled."

"That's because your memory's under a cloud," answered the Donkey Johnnykin; "but it's all

right. We're all going on—going always—boys,
and donkeys, and goblins—each in his own way.
I've got your place—you've got a far better one,
if you only knew it. It'll be long enough before
I ever come up to You, very long. But meanwhile one must live. If you should happen to
want a few pounds now?" he added, with a
good-natured smile.

"Thank you," said Johnnykin, "I have money."

"All right. I might have known that they
who have made me pretty well off wouldn't
leave You poor."

"*They?*" said Johnnykin.

"Yes—and a good lot They are. If you want
to see Them, however," he added, "you'd better
be going. I'd be glad to keep you to dinner,
but there's better company expecting you."

"Where am I to go?" asked Johnnykin.

"To the next village inn."

Johnnykin shook hands with the other Johnnykin and his Uncle, and set out. A feeling was
in his mind as of some good fortune coming.

As he entered the inn, he saw at the door
a very neat, large carriage. The coachman had
an honest face, and it was very like an owl's.
He touched his hat very civilly to Johnnykin, as
if he knew him.

"Where have I seen that man before?" said
Johnnykin.

As he entered the parlour, he found in it
a very queer, little elderly gentleman, and
another much older, with a long beard. The

latter was hearty and joyous-looking, and seemed to be a clergyman. With them were two beautiful young ladies. One of these had golden hair and blue eyes, but the other looked like a Gipsy. As Johnnykin's eyes met theirs, he felt sure he had seen them somewhere before.

He sat down, and the old gentleman cheerfully bade him good day, and began at once to talk of the country about, of the old churches and sketching. Johnnykin offered to be his guide to what he wanted to see.

"And you are an artist. May we look at your sketches?"

The first picture that Johnnykin took out was that of the Goblin.

"Oh, Uncle, it's *so* like you!" cried the dark young lady.

Johnnykin hid his face in his hands. Something like a memory of this, too, came to him. As he raised his eyes, he saw that the young ladies were looking at him as if with pity.

o

While walking out, the Uncle questioned Johnnykin as to his home and life; when he heard from the young man all he knew of himself, and his queer story, he was silent for a time and then said:

"I see. A very curious case, my young friend. I do not doubt in the least what you have told me; but I would like to ask the opinion of my old friend Doctor Bacon. Ah!— here he is!"

Then the Doctor listened to all that Johnnykin could tell. When he had heard it, he said:

"Very interesting. I should like to take a few notes of this case. Well, young gentleman, it so happens that I am in great need of an assistant—particularly of one who can draw. I am going with these friends up to London to perfect some inventions. If you will enter my service, I shall be happy to engage you. I will see that your education is not neglected."

They had come by this time, in their walk, to an old ruined Norman church; and in an odd corner of it was a bench, hard by a fast-running stream. There Johnnykin sat with the young ladies, watching the last orange and red sunset streaks in the Western sky through the trees. He looked at the young lady with the blue eyes, wondering if she could tell him anything about himself, and I suppose he must have looked very pitifully, for she suddenly said:

" It's too cruel! I can't bear this any longer. He really ought to know."

" And I *won't* bear it any longer, either ! " cried the dark young lady. " He has borne the trial like a lamb. I am human now, and I don't mind the old law. Let's tell him all ! "

And as the last light of the setting sun touched his eyes, Johnnykin suddenly remembered Everything, and cried:

" *Marjolaine !* "

Now, do you want to be told how they all went into Life together, and how Johnnykin became a great artist and poet, and how they were all friends to the end ? Do you know, I think that many a man's life among those we meet really conceals as great wonders as were shown to Johnnykin ?

And they really did see Willie Winkie in their house one day in due time. He kept his promise, and made a long visit—in fact, I believe he came several times. I also think from what I hear of the behaviour of some young people, that Chesmé must have invited back to life not only Charley Cake-and-Ale, but Margery Daw, Lazy Tom, Cross-Patch, and several other celebrated persons, of whom you have heard in the Goblin songs of the Nursery, which are used as magic spells to put children to sleep. I suppose that Chesmé did this to reform their ways.

But it is very difficult for some little Goblins to become good.

THE END.

www.ingramcontent.com/pod-product-compliance
Lightning Source LLC
Chambersburg PA
CBHW030254270626
47156CB00022B/2706